Nick leaned back in his seat and rubbed his eyes. Human sacrifices, traps, snakes . . . It sounded like this vacation was going to be a lot more than he had bargained for. "Do you really think the pyramid *we're* going to is cursed?"

Angelo shrugged. "I guess we won't know until we get there. But you remember how your dad said it was discovered fifty years ago? Well, I looked up the group of archaeologists who found the pyramid and started to explore it. They were hoping it was filled with treasure. Then, only a day after they managed to find the entrance, the entire expedition was called off."

"They just decided to go home?" Nick asked. "What about the treasure?"

"They didn't go home," Angelo said, his eyes huge and dark behind his glasses. "They didn't go anywhere. They sent a couple of men back to bring more supplies. But when the men returned, the entire camp was abandoned. No bodies. No notes. Just gone."

To Jack, Lizzie, and Grey,
who have many monster-hunting
days ahead of them

Case File 13 #4: Curse of the Mummy's Uncle
Text copyright © 2015 by J. Scott Savage
Illustrations copyright © 2015 by Douglas Holgate
All rights reserved. Printed in the United States of America.
No part of this book may be used or reproduced in any manner whatsoever
without written permission except in the case of brief quotations embodied in
critical articles and reviews. For information address HarperCollins Children's
Books, a division of HarperCollins Publishers, 195 Broadway, New York, NY
10007.
www.harpercollinschildrens.com

Library of Congress Cataloging-in-Publication Data
Savage, J. Scott (Jeffrey Scott), 1963– author.
    Curse of the mummy's uncle / J. Scott Savage.
        pages   cm. — (Case file 13 ; volume 4)
    Summary: "The three Monsterteers are off on a vacation to Mexico, where
they join an archaeological excavation of an abandoned—and haunted—Mayan
pyramid"— Provided by publisher.
    ISBN 978-0-06-232407-8
    [1. Archaeological expeditions—Fiction. 2. Mayas—Antiquities—
Fiction. 3. Indians of Mexico—Fiction. 4. Supernatural—Fiction. 5. Best
friends—Fiction. 6. Friendship—Fiction. 7. Mexico—Fiction.]   I. Title.
PZ7.S25897Cur   2015   2014034160
[Fic]—dc23   CIP
                                                                               AC

Typography by Sarah Nichole Kaufman
16 17 18 19 20   OPM   10 9 8 7 6 5 4 3 2 1
❖
First paperback edition, 2016

CASE FILE 13

CURSE OF THE MUMMY'S UNCLE

J. SCOTT SAVAGE

HARPER
An Imprint of HarperCollinsPublishers

An Ominous Outing

Warm beaches, a log cabin in the woods, a theme park filled with roller coasters and cotton candy. These are what most people think of when planning their perfect getaway.

Of course, by now I am well aware that you are not *most people*. When you think of beaches, you imagine strange and dangerous creatures lurking beneath the surface of an otherwise calm bay. The thrill of a roller coaster is far too tame for you, and woods are only as interesting as the things that come creeping out late at night.

Nick, Carter, and Angelo are leaving for a vacation that may be right down your alley. A cursed pyramid, oddly named demons, and strange disappearances are only the beginning. I'm afraid I won't be going on this trip. When I fly the night skies I don't use an airplane.

But I've asked a friend to look in on them from time to time and take notes. If you're in the area, please do the same. I'll be sure to update everything that happens right here in Case File 13.

And in the meantime: if you find yourself visited by an (incredibly) old friend, wrapped from head to foot in bandages, don't go crying to your mummy.

CHAPTER 1

AL SER UN NIÑO, SIEMPRE LO SERÁ

ONCE A BOY, ALWAYS A BOY

Nick grabbed his bags, glanced one last time in the mirror to make sure everything was perfect, and headed down the stairs. He still couldn't believe his dad had won an all-expenses-paid trip to Mexico. And if that wasn't awesome enough, they were going to join an archaeology group helping dig out a newly discovered pyramid called Aktun. A name he wasn't sure he could pronounce, but that sounded totally cool anyway. The best part was Nick's two closest friends and fellow Monsterteers, Angelo and Carter, got to come too. Although it meant delaying Christmas for a few days, he couldn't imagine a better way to spend the holidays than looking for mummies.

Whistling the theme song from one of his favorite movies, he jumped the last two steps and headed into the kitchen, where his mom was going over a checklist on her computer. "All packed?" she asked as he dropped his bags next to the back door.

"Checked and doubled." He walked up behind his mom's chair, waiting for her to look at him. But her eyes were locked on the monitor.

"Toothbrush and toothpaste?" Mom asked, hovering her cursor over an item called toiletries.

"Electric, nonelectric in case they don't have outlets we can use, and minty fresh," Nick said.

Mom highlighted the next item on her list. "Swimsuit, water shoes, and shorts?"

"Like a boss." He edged around her chair, hoping she would see him from the corner of her eye.

"A clean pair of underwear for every day?"

"Mom!" He groaned. "Do you really have to ask me about my underwear? It's not like I go around asking you about your . . . you know. *Stuff*." The last way he wanted to start his winter break was talking to his mom about underwear.

"We're going to be in Mexico for a week, and we may not have any place to wash clothes," Mom said in a no-nonsense voice. "It's not my fault boys smell like spoiled bologna after a day of doing whatever it is they do." She pushed back her chair, turned around, and looked him up and down. "What is that on your head?"

Nick grinned, tugged the felt fedora over his forehead, and said in a gruff voice, "It's not the years, honey, it's the mileage."

Mom glared. "Excuse me?"

"It's from *Raiders of the Lost Ark*," Nick said, throwing his hands up in the air. "I can't believe you didn't recognize the quote or the hat."

From the other side of the room came a knock at the door. Nick hurried to answer it, knowing it would be either Carter or Angelo. They'd recognize the hat for sure.

He swung open the door to find Angelo standing outside with his shoulders squared and a sneer on his face. "We do not follow maps to buried treasure, and X never, ever marks the spot," Angelo said, quoting an *Indiana Jones* line.

Nick couldn't believe his eyes. "Who said you could wear a fedora? You are so ripping me off."

Angelo looked just as surprised as Nick felt. "I told you *I* was wearing it. If anyone ripped anyone off, it's you." He grabbed his bags and carried them into the kitchen.

"You did not." Nick couldn't believe they'd both decided to wear their Indiana Jones hats. "What's that?" Nick asked, noticing something new sticking out of the top of his friend's backpack.

"Oh, this?" Angelo looked down casually, as if he hadn't left the piece of equipment sticking out on purpose. Angelo was a total brain. Besides knowing everything there was to know about monsters, monster movies, and anything supernatural, he also invented things. Just a few weeks before, he'd come up with a machine that could track corpses by smell. Nick's dad called Angelo the Smarticle Particle, although Angelo was nearly as tall as an adult.

Angelo unzipped the pack and removed a weird little device the size of a lunch box. It looked like someone had ripped open a toaster, torn the guts from a microwave oven, and combined them with random test tubes and other pieces from a chemistry kit. Proudly he held out the device for Nick's inspection. "I don't want to brag or anything. But you've heard of a DNA sequencer, right?"

"Surrrre," Nick said slowly. Although he thought he'd heard the words before, he wasn't quite as sure he knew what they meant. "DNA is the stuff in your body that decides what color your eyes will be or if you'll have hair all over your back. And a sequencer, um . . . sequences things."

"Close enough." Angelo held out the lunch box thing, clearly proud of his invention. "This isn't a full-on

4

DNA sequencer. That would be crazy. Although I'd like to try making one sometime. This is a thermal cycler that uses a polymerase chain reaction to—"

"Dude!" Nick held out both hands. "Any more of that scientific blibbity-blabber and my head is going to explode—ruining a perfectly good Indiana Jones fedora, which *I* decided to wear long before you ever did. Get to the point. Using sixth-grade words, what does that science fair project on steroids actually do?"

Angelo looked like someone had insulted his baby sister—if he'd had a baby sister to insult. He gave the lunch box a loving pat and sighed. "It tests DNA. Just like the police do when they want to prove who committed a crime."

"Uh huh." Nick bit the tip of his tongue for a second, trying not to hurt his friend's feelings any more than he already had. Like Spider-Man's superpowers, Angelo's genius was both a gift and a curse. "Look, that sounds totally . . . legit. I mean, I couldn't have made something like that in a hundred years. But do you really want to spend our winter break going around testing people's DNA?"

"It's not for testing *people's* DNA," Angelo said, clearly mortified. "I mean, it could. But what would be the point?"

Now Nick was totally confused. "If you're not going

to use it to test people's DNA, whose DNA are you going to test?"

Angelo's eyes gleamed like he'd been waiting for that exact question. "Aliens'!"

Before Nick could respond, the kitchen door flew open, and Carter came bursting through wearing an Indiana Jones hat of his own. "*Verrugas*," he said with a terrified look on his face. "*¿Por qué tengo que tener verrugas?*"

Nick could only shake his head. Was he really going to spend a week in a foreign country with these two? "What in the world are you talking about?"

Carter grinned, tossing a couple of duffel bags onto the kitchen table. "It's Spanish, amigo. It means 'Snakes? Why did it have to be snakes?'"

"Hate to break it to you," Angelo replied, "but that's not what you just said." He would know; his mom was from Puerto Rico and his dad was from Chile. Angelo had been raised speaking both Spanish and English, although his mom usually spoke English when they were around other people.

Nick's mom smiled at Carter. "He's right. What you said was 'Warts. Why do I have to have warts?'"

Nick stared at his mom. "When did *you* learn Spanish?"

6

Mom got up from the desk and flicked the brim of his hat. "My great-grandfather on my father's side was from Mexico. My grandfather taught us all to speak Spanish when we were little. My speaking skills are a little rusty. But I'm positive *verrugas* means warts."

Nick looked at his mom like he was seeing her for the first time. Next thing he knew she'd be telling him she hunted vampires in high school.

"Warts?" Carter yelped. "How can that be? I've been practicing that phrase for weeks." For the first time, he seemed to notice that Angelo and Nick were wearing the same hat as he was. "Hey! You two stole my idea!"

"Stole *your* idea?" Angelo and Nick said at the same time.

"Yeah." Carter frowned. "The Indiana Jones hat is like my trademart. I've been wearing one for as long as I can remember."

"I think you mean trade*mark*," Angelo corrected. "And I've never seen you wear one before. In fact, it looks brand-new."

"I'll bet you don't even remember where Indy got it from," Nick said.

"He took it from Garth, a treasure hunter," Carter snapped back.

"He didn't take it," Nick said. "Garth gave it to him after Indy stole the Cross of Coronado on a scout trip."

"Who cares?" Carter stamped his foot, his face turning red. "*I* look the best in it, and I'm *not* taking it off."

"This is *my* vacation. So that means *I* get to wear it," Nick said.

"We can't all bring it," Angelo said. "We'd look stupid wearing the same thing. Like those kids in the *Sound of Music* movie who had to wear matching clothes made out of curtains."

Nick had no idea what Angelo was talking about. But this was an even worse way to start winter break than discussing underwear with his mother.

Mom took Nick's hat off his head and held out her hands to Carter and Angelo. "I'll settle this argument. None of you are taking the hats. Have any of you considered how childish you'd all seem wearing a costume from some movie on an archaeological excavation? How many tourists do you think show up, trying to look like Indiana Jones?"

Nick looked sheepishly at his friends. It was a pretty dumb thing to fight about. And his mom was probably right. Even though they thought the hats were cool, he guessed they'd make them look like total losers to the real archaeologists. "Okay. I'll leave mine here."

"Me too," Angelo said. "Besides, fedoras aren't nearly as cool on anyone but Indy."

Nick and Angelo looked at Carter.

"Fine!" Carter said, yanking off his hat and slamming it on the table. "But I think I look amazing in it."

"Dude!" Nick said. "What did you do to yourself?" Carter was always dyeing his spiky hair a different color. But this time he'd gone overboard. The left side of his head was green, the right side was red, and the middle was white.

Carter patted his head. "I colored it last night. It's in honor of the Mexican flag."

"Very . . . patriotic," Mom said. She gave her computer one last check before powering it down. "Now, where's your father? We need to get on the road."

A series of footsteps sounded from the stairs and a second later, Nick's dad bounded into the kitchen. He was wearing a felt fedora and a leather jacket. In his right hand was an actual bullwhip. With a wide grin, he held out the whip and said, "Fortune and glory, kids. Fortune and glory!"

9

CHAPTER 2

¿QUIÉN CONSTRUYÓ LAS PIRÁMIDES?

WHO BUILT THE PYRAMIDS?

Dad drove most of the way to the airport with his hands locked on the steering wheel and his lips pressed tightly together.

"You're not still upset that that I wouldn't let you wear your costume, are you?" Mom asked.

"I told you, it wasn't a costume," Dad said, staring straight ahead. "It was a hat to keep the sun out of my eyes, and a jacket to . . . to keep the bugs off."

"I'm sure a heavy leather jacket would be comfortable in the middle of a rain forest," Mom said. "Let me guess—the whip was for mosquitoes?"

Dad glared at her. "Wait until a tiger is running straight for you, lady. Then you'll wish I'd thought to bring a weapon."

"Technically," Angelo said, "tigers live in—"

"Shhh," Nick hissed. He'd seen his mom and dad disagree enough to know that they'd go on like this for a few more minutes. Then one of them would crack a joke. And the next thing you knew, they'd be all lovey-dovey again, like they'd never been arguing. It was one of the things he liked best about his parents. Plus, he wasn't about to mention that he'd seen his dad sneak the whip into his suitcase when Mom wasn't looking.

"I was just going to say that tigers live in Asia," Angelo said softly. "There could be jaguars or pumas where we're going, and plenty of dangerous snakes, but no tigers."

Nick was pretty sure that if his mom overheard Angelo talking about all the dangerous animals they could encounter, this trip would end before it ever got started. So he quickly changed the subject. "What was that you were saying back at the house about aliens?"

As soon as the word *alien* left Nick's mouth, Angelo pulled out his monster notebook. He took the thick binder with him everywhere. It was filled with informa-tion about unusual things they'd seen in the past, and things he thought they might run across in their travels. After all the weird stuff that had happened to them, it was getting almost too thick to carry.

Angelo flipped through the pages until he reached a map of different pyramids with lines drawn from one to the other, and lots of scribbled notes. "A lot of people think most, if not all, of the pyramids were built by aliens. The hieroglyphs carved into the walls could be their writings."

Carter guffawed. "So if you unwrap one of the mummies you'd find little green guys with three arms and antennas? And the hyro-whatchamacallits actually translate into 'Take me to your leader'?"

"Very funny," Angelo said, clearly not amused. "Maybe *you* don't believe it. But scientists still aren't sure how some of the biggest rocks in the pyramids were moved there. And I read somewhere that the mortar used in the Great Pyramid of Egypt is so unusual no one has been able to reproduce it, even with modern technology."

Nick was impressed, but still not convinced. "Why would aliens want to build pyramids?"

"There are lots of theories." Angelo thumbed through the pages. "Landing sites for the spaceships, markers to guide them from space—kind of like lighthouses. Maybe they were used as some sort of interstellar communication towers."

"I don't know," Nick said. "That seems like kind of a stretch."

"Does it?" Angelo sounded unusually edgy. He snapped open a map of an Egyptian pyramid and tapped his finger on a circle. "This is the spot where the Egyptians dug up most of the rocks they used to build the Great Pyramid. Remembering that some of those stones weighed as much as seventy tons, and had to be pushed or pulled to the site without modern machinery, where would you build your pyramid?"

"As close as I could get," Carter said.

"Yeah," Nick added, studying the map. "Somewhere easy to get to. With no hills between it and the—what's the place where you dig called, a quarry?"

"That's what most people would do." Angelo pointed to another spot on the map. "But whoever built the Great Pyramid dragged more than two million stones here, hundreds of miles away—even though there were other locations just as good much closer."

Dad glanced at Angelo in the rearview mirror. "That's all well and good, but we're not going to Egypt. The Mexican pyramids were built by the Mayans."

"Maybe they were and maybe they weren't," Angelo said. He reached over the seat to touch his DNA tester. "The builders of Aktun could have moved it a few miles north or south and chosen a spot much easier to reach. Instead they erected it in the middle of a thick rain forest. Why would they do that?"

"To be near McDonald's?" Carter joked.

Angelo didn't even bother responding to that.

Nick didn't have an answer. And after some of the things they'd seen in their own town during the last couple of months, he wasn't willing to say anything was impossible. "Maybe the pyramids were like huge garages for their spaceships," he suggested. "Do you think we could find evidence of ETs in the pyramid we're going to? Like, you know, alien bodies or flying saucers?"

"I doubt it," Angelo said. "They were too smart to leave much behind. If not, people would have discovered something by now. But they may have left evidence too small to see. Bits of alien skin, or hair, or even blood. That's why I brought my DNA-testing kit. If I can find tissue samples that don't belong to any earthly humans or animals, that would prove ETs were there."

Up front, Dad chuckled. "I don't think you're going to find any aliens. But there are some pretty cool things about the Mexican pyramids. Things that might keep you awake late at night." He said the last part in a creepy-movie voice.

14

"Yeah?" Carter leaned forward in his seat. "What kinds of things?"

Dad glanced at Mom with a mischievous smile. "I don't know if I should tell you. Some of the stories are pretty gory. Your mother might not approve."

"You mean like blood and guts?" Carter asked excitedly. "Tell us. Tell us."

Mom waved her hand. "Go ahead. It can't be any worse than some of the stuff they see on TV."

"Well," Dad said, obviously getting back into a good mood, "you probably know that many of the pyramids were used as burial sites."

Nick had seen plenty of scary movies about pyramids. "Sure. Mummies and treasure and stuff like that."

Dad nodded. "But that wasn't all they were used for. Many Mayans and Aztecs performed rituals that often included human sacrifice."

Nick shivered. "You mean they killed people inside?"

"Not *inside*," Dad said, glancing at the boys in the rearview mirror. "On *top*. They actually painted some of the pyramids red to match the bloodstains. Most of those people were prisoners of war, and criminals. But to appease their gods, some of the victims were—"

"All right," Mom said so loud it made all four boys jump. "I think we've had enough pyramid stories for a while. What if we listen to some nice music for the rest of the drive?"

"Fine by me," Dad said. "I thought they should know that some of those victims are probably still there. Hanging around as ghosts. Aktun was discovered more than fifty years ago. But the government stopped exploration until just recently. Because it's supposed to be *cursed*."

Nick shivered. Even as someone who liked monsters and scary stories, this hit a little too close to home. Were they really going to be entering a pyramid where people had been killed? He could imagine headless corpses coming back to life in the middle of the night to hunt down anyone who dared intrude on their graves.

Now it was Mom's turn to stare at the road. She tuned the radio to classical—Dad's least favorite kind of music—and sat silently next to him.

Angelo glared at his monster notebook, squeezing it until his knuckles turned white. "Just because the Mayans used the pyramids for sacrifices doesn't mean they built them. For all we know the aliens were the ones who started the ceremonies."

Nick shrugged. "Maybe so."

"Not maybe. *Definitely*." Angelo slammed the notebook shut.

Nick looked at him closely. "Is everything okay?"

Angelo seemed on the verge of saying something, then shook his head. "I just really want to prove the existence of extraterrestrials, all right?"

"Sure," Nick said. "Let me know how I can help."

Carter, who had been the most interested in hearing the stories, seemed the least bothered by them. He twisted around in his seat, trying to dig through the luggage in the back. "Can you grab my bag?" he asked Nick. "It's got my Nintendo DS, my PSP, and all my video games in it."

"You brought video games?" Nick asked.

"Yeah. I'd die without them for a whole week. Same goes for my candy stash."

Nick pushed around the suitcases and bags until he found Carter's black bag covered with stickers of various monsters.

"Not that one," Carter said. "That has my clothes and stuff. My games are in the red bag."

"A long one?" Angelo asked. "With a black draw-string?"

Carter nodded. "Yeah. Do you see it?"

"I *saw* it," Angelo said. "On the kitchen table right before we got in the car."

Nick pushed around a couple of bags and shook his head. "I'm not seeing it back here, dude. I think you might have left it behind."

CHAPTER 3

¿PENSASTE QUE TEJER FUERA PARA LAS ABUELAS?

YOU THOUGHT KNITTING WAS FOR GRANDMAS?

"We have to go back. We *havvvve* to!" Carter clasped his hands in front of his chest and begged, even though they were already in line, getting onto the plane. "We can take another flight, or ask the pilot to wait."

"I'm sorry, Carter, but for the last time, we can't," Nick's dad said. "Being without video games for a week will be good for you. When I was a boy we didn't have video games. We didn't even have toys. The rich kids at least had rocks and sticks to hit each other with. We had to throw imaginary rocks at each other and pretend to bleed."

"Ignore him," Nick said. "My dad gets some weird kind of pleasure out of seeing kids suffer. One time our

TV was out for a month and he told me if I needed to watch something, I could bang my head against the wall until I saw stars."

"You don't understand." Carter looked desperately back into the terminal. "I have some kind of allergy. If I don't play video games every day, I get this weird rash on my palms, my feet go all sweaty, and my whole body starts to shake."

Nick patted him on the back, trying to comfort him. "How about if you read a book? I've got a couple in my pack."

"A *book*?" Carter ran both hands through his hair. "Would you offer a man who was dying of thirst a bag of pretzels? You're killing me."

"There's no such thing as a video game allergy," Angelo said, typing something into his iPad.

Carter's eyes fixed on Angelo's tablet. "Dude, please tell me you have games on that thing."

Angelo shook his head at once. "Not a chance. I've been downloading all the information I can find on Mexican pyramids. I've got a ton of research to do. I'm not letting you kill my battery with games."

The five of them reached their seats. Nick's mom and dad sat on one side with an open seat between them, while Nick, Angelo, and Carter slid into the other side. Carter was breathing heavily. "I think I'm going to have an attack or something."

"Maybe they'll have an arcade at the hotel," Nick said.

Carter gasped like a fish flopping about on the bank of a lake. "How, how long . . . is . . . the . . . flight?"

Nick checked his ticket. "Just over eight hours to Mexico City. Then another two hours to . . ." He scratched his head. "How do you say the name of this place? *Tuxtla Gutiérrez*?"

Angelo said something that sounded sort of like *tootsla gooty-erez*. "It's the capital of Chiapas."

"I'm going to have to practice that," Nick said. "Anyway, according to this, we get in just after midnight."

"I can't make it that long," Carter said. "Seriously, guys, I have to get off the plane." He unbuckled his seat belt and started to get up. Before he could stand, Nick's mom reached across the aisle and plopped a light blue ball into his lap. A large metal pin stuck out from one side. "What's this?" Carter asked.

"Yarn and a knitting needle," Mom said. "It's the best relaxation there is."

Carter shoved the ball back toward her. "No way. I'm getting off the—"

"All right," Mom said, taking the yarn. "You probably wouldn't have been good at this game anyway. It's much harder than anything on your Nintendo. I'll bet you couldn't even get past the first level."

Carter paused halfway into the aisle. "It has levels?"

Mom started to put the ball into her bag. "Level one is called Cast On. You get a hundred points if you pass it. Like I said, though, it's probably too hard for you."

"Excuse me," a flight attendant in a dark blue suit said, "we're getting ready to close the door. You have to take your seats now."

Carter looked uncertainly from the front of the plane to the ball. "One hundred points?" he whispered.

"*If* you get past level one," Mom said. "It's not as easy as killing zombies. You have to hold the needle in your right hand and drape a length of yarn over your left thumb and finger."

Almost without Carter even noticing, Mom gently pushed him into his seat and fastened his belt. She handed him the yarn and showed him how to wrap it around his thumb and pull the knitting needle in such a way that the yarn looped around it.

Nick watched, amazed, as his mom walked Carter through creating one loop after another on his needle. "Great job!" she said. "That's fifty points. Keep it up

21

and soon you'll reach level two, Knit Stitch. And you'll earn a second needle."

Carter was so caught up in making his stiches, he didn't notice when the plane pulled away from the terminal and rose into the air.

"Are you watching this?" Nick said, leaning over to Angelo.

"Huh?" Angelo looked up briefly from his tablet, then returned to his reading.

"It's like Carter totally forgot about his video games," Nick whispered, afraid he would break whatever spell his mom had cast on his friend.

"Yeah, that's, um, great," Angelo muttered.

Nick leaned over to get a better view of the screen. "What's that you're reading?"

"There's some pretty amazing stuff about pyramids here," Angelo said. "Did you know there are more pyramids in China than in any other country? They're all over the world. In fact, if you include mound pyramids, they're on every continent but Antarctica. There's even one in the United States."

"No way," Nick said, sure that Angelo was messing with him. He would have heard if there was a pyramid in his own country.

Angelo tilted the tablet so Nick could see a

grass-covered hill with stairs going up the middle of it. "Monk's Mound is located just a few miles from St. Louis, Missouri. It's about the same size as the Great Pyramid of Giza, and historians think it was built over a thousand years ago."

Nick studied the picture. How had he never heard about that?

"That's not all," Angelo said. "What your dad told us about the sacrifices is true. Most of the time, pyramids were used for religious purposes. Many cultures viewed them as a way to communicate with the gods. But some of them were used for human sacrifices." He ran his finger down a line of text and whistled. "Listen to this. In the late 1400s, the Aztecs reconsecrated the Pyramid of Tenochtitlan by sacrificing as many as eighty thousand people in four days."

"That can't be right." Nick tried to the do the math in his head. "That would be like eight hundred people an hour." It sounded like something his dad would make up to scare him.

Angelo blew out his cheeks. "It's true. If you think of all those deaths, it's no wonder so many people believe the pyramids are cursed."

Nick leaned closer to Angelo so his mom couldn't overhear them. "Cursed like . . . ghosts and stuff?"

"Maybe," Angelo agreed. "But also traps, cave-ins, and poisonous snakes. Sometimes people who disturb the resting place of the undead just suddenly have heart attacks and die."

Nick leaned back in his seat and rubbed his eyes. Human sacrifices, traps, snakes . . . It sounded like this vacation was going to be a lot more than he had bargained for. "Do you really think the pyramid *we're* going to is cursed?"

Angelo shrugged. "I guess we won't know until we get there. But you remember how your dad said it was discovered fifty years ago? Well, I looked up the group of archaeologists who found the pyramid and started to explore it. They were hoping it was filled with treasure. Then, only a day after they managed to find the entrance, the entire expedition was called off."

"They just decided to go home?" Nick asked. "What about the treasure?"

"They didn't go home," Angelo said, his eyes huge and dark behind his glasses. "They didn't go anywhere. They sent a couple of men back to bring more supplies. But when the men returned, the entire camp was abandoned. No bodies. No notes. Just gone. The two men were so scared, they ran all the way back to town. The pyramid has been off-limits since then, until just over

24

a month ago when the Mexican government suddenly agreed to a new expedition."

Nick ran his tongue over his suddenly dry lips. "Alien abduction?"

"That's what I'm thinking," Angelo said.

"Or maybe the aliens left some kind of trap. Those explorers could still be inside with their guts sucked out of them. Or maybe they're still alive somehow—all wrapped in bandages and mummified, moaning and groaning to be let out."

Angelo tilted his head. "I wouldn't be surprised." He grabbed his monster notebook and turned to a picture of a shambling corpse covered with brown, scabby-looking bandages. The bandages hung in shreds from the mummy's hands and face, like he'd clawed them open with his own fingers, revealing empty black eye sockets and stumpy brown teeth.

Nick looked from the picture to Angelo. Slowly both the boys began to grin. "This is going to be the coolest vacation ever."

The rest of the flight was fairly uneventful. Nick tried reading one of his books, but even though the story was interesting enough, his mind kept slipping back to what Angelo had said about the first archaeologists to explore the pyramid.

25

They couldn't have been attacked by wild animals or they would have left behind blood and other evidence. Maybe they'd discovered proof of the extraterrestrials and the aliens kidnapped them to hide the truth. He could see the explorers racing out of the pyramid entrance, shaking with excitement about what they had discovered. Then, as they step outside, a huge shadow moves over the pyramid, and a purple tractor beam sucks them all up into the ship like ants through a straw.

He knew one thing for sure. If Mom got sucked up by aliens for exploring this pyramid, she would never forgive Dad for winning this vacation.

He wished he had someone to talk to about his fears, but Angelo was focused on his reading, and Carter had moved across the aisle to sit by Nick's mom. The two of them were flashing their needles back and forth like it was some kind of contest.

"That's awesome," Mom said. "You're a natural. Now we need to learn how to do a purl stitch."

Nick leaned across the aisle. "Dude," he whispered to Carter, "it's nice of you to hang out with my mom, but you really don't have to do that."

Carter frowned. "Your mom's cool."

Nick stared at his friend, wondering if the altitude

had done something to his brain. "Don't you think a kid our age knitting is kind of . . . *weird*? It seems more like something a grandma would do."

Carter slowly set down his knitting needles, eyes narrowed almost to slits. "You're just jealous that she taught me and not you."

"I am not." Nick twisted his paperback. He wasn't jealous, was he? Sure, he was surprised to learn his mom spoke Spanish and had never told him about it. And now she was teaching his best friend to knit when she'd never offered to teach him.

He scowled at Carter. "Fine. Just don't blame me if your skin turns pruny and you start talking about the days before they had color television."

Carter sneered. "Go back to your reading."

Nick leaned over to Angelo. "Don't you think it's kind of weird that my best friend and my mom are knitting together?"

Angelo looked up from his tablet. "Have you ever heard of something called the *Popol Vuh*?"

"The purple what?"

"It's an ancient Mayan text about the creation of man, and this place called Xibalba, which is supposed to be the underworld. Only what if Xibalba isn't the underworld at all? What if it's really a . . ." Angelo's voice trailed off and his eyes got a faraway look as he returned to his reading.

Nick sighed. Out of all the kids in the world he could have brought on vacation, he'd ended up with one who wanted to be knitting buddies with his mom and another who was about as fun as a department-store mannequin. Maybe next time he'd invite Angie and her friends—the girls who were always trying to one-up Nick, Carter, and Angelo on their monster hunts. At least they'd be interesting to argue with.

CHAPTER 4

EL HOTEL
NO ME OFRECE
COMIDA GRATIS

MY HOTEL
DOESN'T GIVE
ME FREE FOOD

By the time they got off their last flight, Angelo's eyes were too bleary to read, Carter's fingers were too tired to knit, and all Nick could think about was a warm bed.

Mom covered a huge yawn with her hand as they stumbled off the plane. "Is everything okay?" she asked Nick. "You've been awfully quiet."

Nick grunted. How did you tell your mother that it was kind of weird realizing you didn't know everything about her, and wondering what else you didn't know? "Just tired, I guess."

"Where are we staying?" Carter asked. "I hope it has a buffet."

"That's a good question." Mom looked at Dad. "You

never did tell me where our hotel is."

"We're explorers. The world is our hotel," Dad said, trying to crack a joke, but Mom wasn't having any of it. "I'm not actually sure where we're staying," he admitted. "The brochure wasn't very big on details."

"You mean we might not have *anywhere* to stay?" Nick asked. The idea that they were in a foreign country after midnight and they could possibly be stranded was too terrifying to consider. "What if no one even knows we're here? What if we have to spend the night in the airport? What if they kick us out on the street?"

"We're not spending the night in the airport," Dad said. "Although, if we do, I want to sleep on the baggage carousel. I've always thought it would be kind of fun to go around and around. Very relaxing."

No one was amused.

"Look." Angelo pointed to a guy with a sign as they started down the escalator. The man wore a dark suit and was nearly as wide as he was tall. The sign read BRAITHWAITE, printed in big blue letters.

"Tell me you're here for us," Mom said.

"*Sí, sí.*" The man gave them a huge grin. "*Señor y Señora Braithwaite*? I take you to your hotel."

Nick felt an overwhelming sense of relief as the man helped them gather their luggage and load it

30

into a long black limousine.

"Check this out," Carter said as they piled into the back of the car. "There's a TV." He grabbed the remote, turned on the TV, and began flipping through the channels. "Hey. They're all in Spanish."

Angelo rolled his eyes. "You were expecting Japanese, maybe?"

Dad stretched out on the leather seat and sighed. "This is the life. Didn't I tell you we'd be traveling in style?"

"As I recall," Mom said, "you wanted to sleep with the suitcases." She leaned forward to speak with the driver. "*¿Nos alojamos en un hotel esta noche?*"

The driver nodded back enthusiastically. "*Sí.*"

The two of them spoke back and forth in rapid Spanish, and again, Nick was blown away that she could speak a language he didn't understand. "What are they saying?" he asked Angelo.

"She asked if we're staying at a hotel tonight. He said we're staying at a fancy place called El Cisne Elegante, which means 'the Elegant Swan.' He says it has a swimming pool, hot tubs, golfing, and all kinds of other stuff."

Dad sat up. "Golfing? I used to be quite good with the clubs. Could have gone pro if I'd wanted. Unfortunately I got into trouble when I struck a woman in the head

31

with a badly hit three-iron. Knocked out her glass eye. But even then, the eyeball rolled across the green and straight into the hole. The judges couldn't decide whether to kick me off the course or give me a hole-in-one." The three boys ignored his story completely and he went back to resting.

"Do they have a restaurant?" Carter asked, always ready for something to eat.

"Yeah," Angelo said. "And according to what the driver was telling your mom, all our expenses are covered. Which means we can eat as much as we want."

"All we can eat?" Carter patted his stomach. "I am in heaven."

The next morning, after a good night's sleep, Nick, Carter, and Angelo headed down to the restaurant with Nick's mom and dad. The hotel was every bit as luxurious as their driver had promised. Soft red and gold carpet covered the floor, except for the lobby and dining areas, which were tiled in huge marble squares. Paintings of Mexican villages and jungle scenes covered the walls. Their suite had two rooms with big-screen TVs and private bathrooms.

"I could get used to this," Mom said as they got off the elevator.

Dad beamed. "I may be a little forgetful at times, but when I book a hotel, I do it right. I told them, 'Spare no expense. Only the best will do for my family.'"

Carter eyed the dining room, where servers were carrying plates of delicious-smelling food. "I could get used to *that*!"

"*Garçon*," Dad said to the man at the door of the restaurant, "may we get a table for five?"

"*Garçon* is French," Mom whispered. "And it means 'boy.'"

The host seated them at a table near the window. Looking out at the sparkling blue water of the pool, Nick couldn't wait to go swimming. But first, breakfast. He was starving.

The menu was written in both Spanish and English. Most of the items were familiar, but a few of them, like chorizo and carne asada, he didn't recognize. When the waitress came to take their order, Nick decided to try the *chilaquiles y huevos*, which the English translation described as corn tortillas smothered with red chili sauce, cheese, and green onions, and topped with eggs.

One by one, they went around the table, until it was Carter's turn. Folding his menu on the table, he smiled and said, "*Me quedo como un cerdo llevando un sombrero tonto.*"

The waitress blinked. "Excuse me?"

Carter licked his lips and tried again, pronouncing each word carefully. *"Me quedo como un cerdo llevando un sombrero tonto."*

The woman taking their order put a hand to her mouth and giggled.

"What do you *think* you're saying?" Angelo asked.

Carter gritted his teeth. "I said I'd like to try one of everything. My sister helped me memorize a list of important Spanish phrases. I've been practicing for weeks."

Angelo couldn't help smiling. "Um, I think your sister was messing with you. What you actually said was 'I look like a pig in a dumb hat.'"

Carter's face went bright red.

"He'll have the same thing as me," Nick said.

As soon as the waitress left, still laughing, Mom turned to Dad and Carter. "From now on neither of you is to try saying anything in Spanish. Is that understood?"

Both of them nodded.

CHAPTER 5

ALÓJESE EN EL HOTEL

STAY AT THE HOTEL

As Nick's family and friends finished breakfast and got up from the table, a group of tourists came through the front door of the hotel, filling the lobby.

"Who wants to go swimming?" Nick asked.

Dad practiced swinging an imaginary golf club. "I'm heading out to the course."

"I'm getting a massage," Mom said. "My back still aches from all those hours on the plane. Then maybe a pedicure."

Someone bumped into Nick and hurried past. Nick turned to see who it was, but the man disappeared into the crowd of tourists without an apology.

"¡Discúlpame!" called the waitress who had served

them their food. She approached Nick and Angelo and handed them a black folder. "Excuse me, but you left this on the table," she said in hesitant English.

"That's not ours," Nick said. But she seemed insistent.

"Yes. On table."

Angelo took the folder and looked at the papers inside.

"What is it?" Nick asked.

Angelo flipped through the pages, his eyes growing wide. "It's a whole bunch of newspaper articles about the original group who entered the pyramid."

Nick looked at the documents, but they were all written in Spanish. "Where did they come from?"

"Someone must have left them for us," Carter said.

But who? The folder hadn't been on the table when they got up from eating, which meant someone had to have put it there right after they left. Someone who—

"The guy who just pushed past me," Nick said. "He left right after we did."

"What did he look like?" Angelo asked.

Nick shook his head. "I didn't really see him."

"Are you boys going swimming?" Mom asked.

"Sure," Nick said. "Do you want to come?"

"That's okay. I really do need that pedicure," Mom said.

"If you are the family I think you are, there won't

36

be time for that," said a dusty-looking little man with a bald head and wire-rim glasses. "You wouldn't happen to be the Braithwaites, would you?"

Dad, who was halfway to the elevator, returned. "Who are you?"

"Hector Jiménez," said the man, popping out a gnarled hand. "Dr. Canul sent me to pick you up. He wanted to get you back to the camp by breakfast, but I'm afraid I got a flat tire on the way. Some of these roads are brutal."

"But I'm going golfing," Dad said.

"And I'm heading back for more breakfast," Carter added.

"No, no, no. I'm afraid that's not possible." Mr. Jiménez waved his hands. "You have a busy day. We need to get you into your tents, show you around the camp, and get you started on the dig."

"Tents?" Mom's face went white. "You mean we aren't staying *here*?"

Mr. Jiménez rubbed his shiny head. "Why would you? The site we're going to is in the Lacandon Jungle, which is over four hours away. And that's when the roads aren't washed out, the bridges are above water, and a herd of cows isn't blocking the way."

Dad looked from Mom to Mr. Jiménez. "Who wants to do boring things like golf and getting your toenails

37

painted when you can risk washed-out roads, under-water bridges, and rampaging cows? Am I right?"

The only person who seemed remotely to be in agreement was Angelo. But by the way his friend was focused on the newspaper articles in the folder, Nick wasn't sure he was even listening all the way.

"Excellent," Mr. Jiménez said, clapping his hands. "I'll pull the car up while you get your luggage."

By the time they had repacked their suitcases and carried them to the front of the hotel, Mr. Jiménez was waiting in an old four-wheel-drive. Unlike the fancy limousine that had picked them up at the airport, this car was muddy and covered with dents and rust.

Carter grimaced. "I'm guessing this thing doesn't have a TV in it."

Nick eyed their pile of luggage. "I don't think we're all going to be able to fit in there."

"Nonsense." Mr. Jiménez grabbed the nearest suitcase—which happened to belong to Nick's mom—and, with surprising strength for a man of his size, threw it on top of the tall car. "Jump to it, boys," he called, grabbing another bag.

Nick, Carter, and Angelo each began handing the luggage to Mr. Jiménez, who tossed the heavy suitcases like they were footballs.

"Can I give you a hand?" Dad asked.

"No need," Mr. Jiménez said. He threw the last bag on top of the car, then strapped them all down with a long rope.

Mom put her hands on her hips and studied the pile of suitcases. "Are you sure those will stay up there? I'm afraid some of them might fall off on the drive."

Mr. Jiménez pinched his lower lip and raised an eyebrow. "It's possible. Hopefully we won't lose anything you need." He climbed behind the wheel of the old car and started it up. A cloud of thick black smoke belched from the exhaust pipe.

Dad gave a weak grin, and Mom sighed. "Tell me again why I let you talk me into this?"

The ride from the hotel to the site of the pyramid was every bit as bumpy and jarring as Mr. Jiménez had predicted. Dad sat in the front passenger seat. Mom and Carter sat in the middle row, where the bumpy road made their knitting next to impossible. Nick and Angelo were in the way back.

"How many other people will be there?" Mom asked. "Tourists, I mean. Like us."

"You five are the only ones," Mr. Jiménez said as he swerved to avoid a pothole that looked big enough to break an axle. "You're quite lucky. No other outsiders

39

have been allowed at this site."

"Are *you* a local?" Dad asked. "Your English is excellent."

Mr. Jiménez chuckled. "Born and raised right here in Chiapas. It was a good life. But we were very poor. Every day I swore I would get out as soon as I could. I applied for and was accepted to the archaeology program at Berkeley."

"That's near where we live," Carter said.

Jiménez honked and waved at a man selling fruit from the back of a truck. "So what did I do as soon as I graduated? Came straight back home to the city I swore I would leave."

"How come no outsiders are allowed at the pyramid?" Nick asked.

The driver studied him in the rearview mirror. "You mean you don't know?"

Nick glanced at Angelo. "Do you?" Angelo had been reading about the pyramid almost nonstop since they left home. If anyone would know, he would.

Angelo reluctantly put down the folder he'd been going through. "Well, first, Aktun isn't actually one pyramid at all. It's two. The pyramid of the sun and the pyramid of the moon."

"*Two*?" Nick stared at Angelo, unable to believe his

40

friend had been holding out on him. "Dude, why didn't you tell me? That's like twice as cool."

Behind the wheel, Mr. Jiménez watched the boys with a dark curiosity. "Very good."

"That's not even the half of it," Angelo said, in the same voice he used to get A-pluses on his oral reports at school. "A lot of people around here believe these pyramids are the original temples of Xpiyacoc and Xmucane."

"I think that's the stuff I rub between my toes to cure athlete's foot," Dad said. Their driver frowned, clearly not amused.

"In Mayan mythology, Xpiyacoc and Xmucane were the god and goddess who created the earth and everything on it," Angelo said. "They are some of the oldest gods of Mayan legend, and are extremely sacred. If these are their temples, it's possible they could be filled with gifts of untold value."

"Gifts?" Carter said, perking up. "You mean, like, treasure and stuff?"

Nick's dad whistled. "No wonder the archaeologists want to open them up."

Mr. Jiménez laughed. "Of course we all dream of finding lost treasures. Alas, those stories have never been verified. Realistically, if there ever was treasure, it was stolen long ago by Spanish explorers or looters."

"That's not what the first archaeologists were most interested in, anyway," Angelo said.

Nick raised an eyebrow. "You're saying they *didn't* want the gold?" He'd seen a lot of mummy movies, and in every one of them, the people exploring the pyramids were hoping to get rich. That's usually what got them in trouble.

"I'm not saying they wouldn't have taken it if they'd had the chance," Angelo said. "But writing found on the outside of the pyramid of the sun claimed a king was buried there. The king's parents died when he was a baby, leaving him to be raised by his aunt and uncle. And apparently, they were holding something of unimaginable power for him. *That's* what the archaeologists were looking for, if you ask me. Not mere gold."

Mr. Jiménez's hands jerked on the wheel, making the car swerve. "Where did you hear all that?"

Angelo slipped the black folder inside his monster notebook. "It was reported in the local newspapers. Fifty years ago, there was a lot of interest in what that item of power might be, and ever since that failed expedition, a lot of people have wanted to go find it. But until this year, the government refused to let anyone go back in. And I know why. I know what the king's aunt and uncle were holding for him."

Jiménez wiped the back of his hand across his mouth. "No one knows that."

Angelo waited a moment, seeming to enjoy the suspense. He tapped something between his feet, and Nick realized it was the DNA tester. "Remember how I told you that Mayans believed Xpiyacoc and Xmucane were the gods who created the world? What if they weren't gods at all, but, instead, came from another realm so advanced the Mayans only *thought* they were gods?"

Whatever point Angelo had been trying to make, Nick wasn't sure he got it. "If they weren't gods, what were they?" He glanced down at the DNA tester, and suddenly it all came together. "You think they were *aliens*."

Angelo's head bobbed up and down enthusiastically. "It all makes sense. Aktun is the modern name of the pyramid. It means 'cave' in Mayan. But originally it was called *Ximasutal*, which is short for *Xma' Su'tal Hats'utsil*. In Mayan, *Xma' Su'tal Hats'utsil* means 'abandoned beauty.' The aliens named it that because they abandoned the beauty of the rain forest to return to their home planet. But what if the aliens left something behind? Something so sacred and powerful, only the king's guardians knew about it?"

Nick could hardly believe what he was hearing. "So the mummy's uncle was protecting . . ."

Angelo looked up to the sky. "A way to bring back the extraterrestrial ship."

CHAPTER 6

NO ESCUCHARON

THEY DIDN'T LISTEN

The first person to break the silence was Mr. Jiménez. Laughing so hard that his glasses bounced around on the tip of his nose, he shook his head. "You Americans watch too many movies." He held one hand up to his ear. "*E.T. phone home. E.T. phone home.* Such an imagination you have."

Angelo glared at the man, his face going white. "You're saying I'm *wrong*?"

Nick couldn't ever remember seeing his friend so offended. He was really into his alien theory.

Mr. Jiménez pulled a handkerchief from the pocket of his khaki shorts and patted at his eyes. "I'm sorry," he said. "I shouldn't have laughed. *Xma' Su'tal Hats'utsil does* translate loosely to 'abandoned beauty.' And, while there is still so much we don't know, the pyramids may very well have been temples to Xpiyacoc and Xmucane."

"Gods who *could* have been aliens," Nick said, feeling like he needed to defend his friend.

Mr. Jiménez waved a hand dismissively. "You've heard of Zeus, Medusa, and Cerberus, yes? According to myth, they were gods too. Does that mean there are really aliens who throw lightning bolts, have snakes for hair, and look like a three-headed dog? They are only stories. Stories told by people long ago to try to explain a world they didn't understand."

Nick had to admit the man made a pretty good point. He loved Greek mythology. But that didn't make it real.

"Trust me," Mr. Jiménez said. "I've studied Mexican archaeology my whole life. If there was even a hint of your . . . *extraterrestrials*, I would know about it."

"What about the king and his aunt and uncle?" Dad asked. "Could they be real?"

Mr. Jiménez tapped him on the chest. "Now you are thinking like a historian. It is quite possible their tombs are somewhere inside the pyramids. As you Americans are fond of saying, where there is smoke, there is often fire. It's even possible there was an important item they were protecting. A trinket probably, with some sort of religious importance. Unfortunately, what little information we have comes from secondhand reports. All photographs and journals were lost when the original camp was attacked."

Nick leaned forward in his seat. "Is that what you think happened to the first archaeologists? They were attacked?"

"What else?" Mr. Jiménez said. "You think they were whisked into space by your *aliens*? No, it was an attack. That's the reason the government has kept the site closed. No conspiracy there."

Nick didn't want to admit that a conspiracy was exactly what he had been thinking. "It's just . . . there was no evidence. Wouldn't animals have left blood or something?"

"There are many dangers in the jungle," Mr. Jiménez said, meeting Nick's eyes. "Not all of them walk on four legs. And not all snakes slither on their bellies."

Nick wasn't sure exactly what that meant. But it didn't sound good. There was one more question he felt like he had to ask. "My dad said the pyramids are cursed. Is that true? Or is it just another myth?"

He expected their driver to laugh like he had at the

47

idea of aliens. Instead he frowned. "I believe I have said enough for now. Perhaps you can ask Dr. Canul when we reach the camp."

Angelo stared silently at the monster notebook in his lap, his lips pressed together.

"Sorry he shot down your alien theory," Nick said.

"He didn't," Angelo said. "Just because he went to college that doesn't make him an expert. Besides, he's not the one in charge of the dig. Dr. Canul is. The doctor's the one who got permission to return to the site. If there's someone who knows what's really inside the pyramids, it's him."

The rest of the drive was fairly quiet. Dad stretched out in his seat and fell asleep—his snoring getting louder and louder until Mom finally reached around the seat and poked him in the ribs.

Nick stared out the window. Once they left the city, the countryside consisted primarily of valleys, villages, and fields. Most of the houses they passed were small, with men in shorts and long white shirts and women in colorful skirts standing outside or working in the fields. A few of them looked up as the car passed by, and Nick waved. Many of the people smiled and waved back.

Over time, the valleys turned to small mountain

ranges, and the fields were replaced by forests so thick Nick had never seen anything like them. Brightly colored birds filled the trees, and once he could swear he saw a monkey with curious dark eyes watch them drive beneath the branch it was perched on.

Despite his big breakfast, Nick's stomach was rumbling by the time Mr. Jiménez turned off onto a muddy road so narrow the trees and bushes on each side scraped against the car.

As the tires bounced and jostled over the uneven ground, Nick's dad woke up with a snort. "Are we there?" he asked, rubbing his eyes and looking around.

Mr. Jiménez shifted the vehicle into low gear and started up a hill so steep Nick didn't think they were going to make it. Mom dropped her knitting and grabbed the handle above her door with a concerned look. But a moment later they reached the top of the hill safely, and six or seven trucks and cars, along with twice that many tents, came into view.

At the sound of the arriving car, several men stepped out from one of the larger tents. Two of the men waved, but the third—a tall man with weathered skin and a dark, V-shaped beard—only glared.

Nick couldn't wait to get out of the car and stretch his legs. As soon as the doors were opened, though, the heat and humidity hit him. After the air-conditioned interior of the car, the rain forest felt like stepping straight into a hot shower. His shirt began sticking to his back before he even got out.

Angelo took off his glasses to wipe away the fog that had formed on the lenses.

After the humidity, the second thing Nick noticed was the noise. From all around them came a constant blast of chirping, buzzing, and tweeting—as though the trees were filled with thousands of tiny violinists and horn players. Clouds of insects swarmed the air around their heads and faces.

"This will take some getting used to," Mom said, slapping at her arms.

One of the men from the tent hurried over with a can and said something in Spanish. Mom closed her eyes and raised her hands as the man sprayed her arms, legs, and face. "It's insect repellent," she said as the man sprayed each of them. "He says it's much stronger than the stuff we brought with us."

"Don't worry about me," Carter said. "I've got my own insect repellent. It's called stinky gas."

The man spraying them must have understood. He smiled and fired off more quick Spanish that made Nick's mom laugh.

"What did he say?" Carter asked.

Angelo grinned. "He said the jaguars like to eat smelly boys."

Nick felt another little twinge of jealousy that his mom and his friend shared something he didn't.

As the men began untying their luggage, Mr. Jiménez led them toward the tents. "Allow me to show you around."

Nick noticed Angelo quickly shove his papers and DNA tester into his backpack. "Don't mention anything about my equipment," Angelo whispered. "I don't want them to know what I'm doing until I get my results." Apparently Mr. Jiménez hadn't discouraged him from his theory.

"Here is the dining area," Mr. Jiménez said, leading them to a large tent. Through the mesh-covered door, Nick could see a heavyset man working over several hissing gas stoves. "Breakfast is served promptly at seven. Lunch and dinner are a little more flexible. You eat when you can, depending on your work schedule."

"Tell me we didn't miss lunch," Carter said, sniffing the air.

"I'm afraid you did," Mr. Jiménez said. "But Dr. Canul has something special planned for you for dinner."

He led them past several smaller canvas structures

51

that didn't smell nearly as appetizing. "These are the latrines. I'm afraid there are no flushing toilets. So make sure and sprinkle a little lime dust when you're done."

"Only the *best*?" Mom whispered under her breath to Dad. Dad pretended to be fascinated by a large red bird in a nearby tree.

"This is where you will sleep." Mr. Jiménez opened the flap of a yellow tent that looked like it was made of some kind of heavy-duty plastic. "It can rain quite hard here. So you'll want to be sure and get under cover when it starts to come down."

Dad stuck his head inside. "There are five cots in here. We won't all be sleeping together, will we?"

"I'm afraid so." Mr. Jiménez chuckled. "Unless you're planning on sleeping outside." He pulled a rope and a plastic divider dropped down the middle of the tent. "Not ideal for a romantic getaway. But it should provide some privacy."

He waved to the tents the men had come out of. "These are where we work. Cleaning, sorting, mapping, storage, that sort of thing. You'll be shown where to go depending on what jobs you are assigned."

"What do you mean, jobs?" Carter said. "I thought this was a vacation."

"A working vacation," Mr. Jiménez said. "Everyone

here has to pull their weight. If you wanted to sit around and sip drinks with little umbrellas, you should have gone on a cruise."

Mom frowned at Dad, and this time he couldn't look away fast enough to keep from meeting her eyes.

Nick looked from the cars to the tents, then past them to the dark green of the rain forest. "Um, aren't we missing something here?"

Mr. Jiménez rubbed the darkly tanned skin of his head. "What did I forget?"

"Only the whole reason we came," Nick said. "Where are the pyramids?"

"An excellent question," said a deep voice.

Nick turned to find the tall man who'd glared at them when they arrived staring down his long nose. Nick felt his skin go cold as the man's unblinking eyes fixed on him.

"Everyone," Mr. Jiménez said, "please meet Dr. Canul."

CHAPTER 7

¿QUÉ MALDICIÓN?

WHAT CURSE?

Dr. Canul's face was so dry and leathery it looked more like beef jerky than skin. His eyes were hard, ebony orbs set deep in his head, and the beard poking out from the tip of his chin was so wispy, it looked more like fungus than hair. If a mummy were pulled out of its tomb, unwrapped, and propped in a corner, Nick thought it would look more lifelike than the man standing in front of him.

"You are the family *fortunate* enough to win a trip to my excavation," the doctor said, looking at the five of them the way an exterminator might look at a nest of especially pesky rats.

"I chose it," Nick's dad said. "I could have picked a

cruise to the Bahamas, a beach resort, or a theme park. But I wanted to come here."

"*Splendid.*" Dr. Canul pinched the bridge of his nose, as though he'd been struck with an extremely bad headache. He waved toward Mr. Jiménez. "Fetch me five hard hats." Mr. Jiménez hurried to a tent and back with an armful of what looked like bright yellow construction helmets.

Dr. Canul handed them each a hard hat. "You will wear these at all times while on the site. I have a great deal of work to do, but I promised I'd show you around. So . . ." He waved his hands—like spiders dying in the air—and walked away.

Nick and his family stared at one another, not sure what to do, before hurrying after the man.

"As you may or may not be aware," Dr. Canul said in a dry, expressionless voice, "Aktun was discovered in the late 1950s by a group of natives. They had no idea what they'd stumbled across. A few stones, a vase, a statue or two. They thought it was nothing more than another in a long line of ancient ruins, until Dr. Samuel Canul heard rumors and realized what the find might actually mean."

"*Canul,*" Nick said. "Was he . . ."

"My father," Dr. Canul said. "I come from a long line

of noted archaeologists." He began climbing up a steep, rocky slope covered with vines, ferns, and moss. "Of course, my father recognized at once that the ruins were, in point of fact, quite possibly one of the greatest finds of the last thousand years. Without putting too fine a point on it, they could be to Mexico what Giza is to Egypt."

Nick rolled his eyes. Clearly the man had a seriously inflated ego. "No offense," he said, trying to keep up, "but isn't that a little bit of an exaggeration?"

Dr. Canul stopped halfway up the hill and spun around, brows pulled so low that his eyes looked like twin caves dug into his face. "It most certainly is not. Do you realize that we could be uncovering the temples of two of the most powerful gods in Mayan lore? The secrets hidden here could unlock clues revealing that my ancestors were the most advanced civilization in the world."

Angelo opened his notebook. "Are you saying you're related to the Mayans who built Xma' Su'tal Hats'utsil?"

Dr. Canul raised his chin. "Not just related. I am a direct descendant of Mayan royalty."

Nick's mother and father caught up with the rest of the group, huffing and gasping for air. "Do we really need to climb all the way to the top?" Dad asked. "We're still adjusting to the elevation."

"No, you do not," Dr. Canul said. "You may go back

anytime you want. In fact, feel free to return to wherever it is you came from. It certainly won't bother me." He turned and began climbing again.

"Maybe you guys should go down and rest," Nick said.

Mom put her hands on her hips and charged up after the archaeologist. "If that pompous, pointy-nosed dirt digger thinks I can't keep up with him, he's got a big surprise coming."

Dad bent over and sucked in a big breath before following her. "What she said."

Nick, Carter, and Angelo hurried after the doctor. "What kinds of secrets do you think are buried here?" Angelo asked.

Dr. Canul tugged the straggly hairs on the end of his chin. "We've barely uncovered a fraction of this site, and already we've discovered that these pyramids and the structures surrounding them are a calendar so precise, it is as accurate as anything we have today. We've also discovered a temple, an amphitheater designed to stage elaborate religious ceremonies, and a star chart tracking everything from the cycles of the moon to the winter and summer equinoxes."

He stopped at the top of the hill near a large, flat rock and turned to look at a stone building several yards away.

"I think you left something out," Angelo said.

Dr. Canul's dark eyes fastened on him. "What would that be?"

Angelo walked to the flat stone, set his backpack on top of it, and said, "Aktun also happens to be the site of some pretty bloody sacrifices."

Nick was barely listening. He'd assumed they'd hiked all this way to reach the pyramids. But other than the flat rock and the stone building, there was nothing to see. "What was the point of coming up here?" he asked, searching all around. "Where are the pyramids?"

Dr. Canul smirked. "You're standing on one of them." He waved a hand. "Welcome to the pyramid of the sun."

It took Nick a minute to understand what the doctor was saying. In his mind, he'd been picturing the Mayan pyramids to look just like the Egyptian pyramids he'd seen in hundreds of movies and images—huge, smooth stones piled up like a giant's building blocks. It had never occurred to him that Aktun might be covered in centuries' worth of plants and dirt.

Once he realized that, it became clear that they had just climbed one of the very pyramids he'd been searching for. The hill opposite them had to be the second

58

pyramid. Nick looked at the space they were standing on, now seeing how flat and uniform it was. Which meant the stone Angelo was standing beside was . . .

"That's an *altar*, isn't it?" he said, walking closer. "One of those things they did sacrifices on."

"Among other things," Dr. Canul spat. "And I would appreciate it if you would remove your backpack from a very sacred pedestal." Angelo grabbed his backpack in a hurry.

Nick looked at the square stone building at the center of the pyramid. It looked about the size of a small stone house, with pillars around the sides and a high, elaborately carved stone roof. "What's that place?"

"A temple," Angelo said. He pointed to a smaller building on the pyramid across from them. "That's another one."

Dr. Canul arched an eyebrow. "At least one of you appears to have a modicum of intelligence."

A few minutes later, Mom reached the top, pulling Dad by the hand. "Come on, you hunk of manly stamina," she said. "One more step and you can take a break."

"Break?" Dad said, wheezing and coughing. "More like a heart attack." As soon as he reached the top, he dropped like a sack of mashed potatoes. "All I have to say is, we better not be going anywhere for the rest of this trip. Because I'm not moving."

"Guess what," Nick said, hurrying over. "We're on the top of one of the pyramids." He pointed to the stone. "That's an altar where they sacrificed people. And that thing over there is a temple."

"I'm not surprised," Dad said. "After climbing to the top of this, I'd be begging them to put me out of my misery."

"What about mummies?" Carter asked. "Have you found any of those? If you did, I hope you didn't bring them back to life. They're almost as bad as vampires. Except they smash your head instead of sucking your blood."

Dr. Canul rolled his eyes.

"Let's look around," Angelo said. He, Nick, and Carter walked across the top of the pyramid to the temple. Unlike the rest of the pyramid, the temple walls were meticulously clean.

"Someone spent a lot of time washing these down," Angelo said, studying the intricate carvings that covered the building's outer and inner walls.

"What's the point?" Nick asked. "I thought all the valuable stuff was inside."

"It is. But these carvings are actually ancient Mayan writing. They had a very advanced language." He tapped one section of the wall. "Some of these are pictures. But these symbols spell actual words. I haven't had a chance to study it as much as I'd like. But I think this means 'power.'"

Carter moved down to an elaborate picture that took up nearly one entire wall. "Who's this little dude on the tiger-skin rug?"

Angelo and Nick walked over to take a look. "It's jaguar skin. And see the scepter he's holding? I think that's part of the ascension ritual they did when a prince became king. But this one's still fairly young. That's how the archaeologists must have figured out that his mother and father were killed."

Angelo traced his finger along a picture of a cave leading to a river. "That's the river of the dead that leads to the underworld. In the *Popol Vuh*, rivers in the underworld were filled with blood or pus."

"Nasty," Carter said. "But also kind of cool."

Angelo studied the pictures. "So these people in the boat must have been his mom and dad who died. And the people standing by the jaguar skin are his aunt and uncle. The item they were guarding was supposed to be so powerful it could help you get past the undead after you died, so you could become a god." He grinned. "But if my theory is right, the item was actually an interplanetary communicator and—"

Before he could finish what he was going to say,

Nick's mom called them. The group stepped out of the temple to find two men laying a blanket and several baskets on the ground.

Carter sniffed. "Wait, is that food I smell?"

The men opened the basket and took out massive quantities of food. Saliva filled Nick's mouth and his stomach growled at the aroma of roasted meat and baked bread. Even Nick's dad managed to pull himself to his feet as the men laid out plates of cheese, fresh fruit, and roasted pork, along with thick slices of what had to be homemade bread.

As they dug into the meal, the food seemed to mellow out Dr. Canul. "There's something about this place," he said, leaning back on his elbow as the sun dropped lower in the western sky. "At times I think I can feel the energy of my ancestors flowing through me."

Nick was afraid of getting his head bitten off by the cranky doctor again, but he couldn't help himself. "Mr. Jiménez said we should ask you about the curse. Do you think it's real?"

The doctor's eyes narrowed. "The greatest secrets have a way of . . . protecting themselves."

"Do you think that's what happened to your father?" Nick asked. "Did he discover some kind of secret?"

"Nick!" Mom said. "That's rude."

Dr. Canul raised his hand. "I do not know what

62

happened to my father. He had some . . . *difficulties* in his later years. But Aktun is a place of power. It would be wise to be careful around it."

Everyone nodded.

"My ancestors believed that after royalty were buried, they traveled a path through the underworld to return to the gods they were descended from. What we see as a pyramid, they saw as a mountain with a cave dug into it. The cave was the entrance to the underworld. The young king buried here was no doubt a powerful person to have two such great pyramids built for him. If there is a curse on this site, it was no doubt placed here by his aunt and uncle, who, from what we've learned, were charged with protecting him."

"The curse of the mummy's uncle," Dad said, grinning. "I like it!"

"Do not take my warning lightly." Dr. Canul stared at each of them. He stood and stretched. "It's time to return to your tents." He turned to speak to the boys directly. "Night is when the jungle's greatest predators come out to hunt. Jaguars, wild boar, boa constrictors. I cannot warn you strongly enough, between sunset and sunrise do not leave your tents under any circumstances. Or you may not return."

CHAPTER 8

ME PARECE COMO
UNA MALA IDEA

THIS SEEMS
LIKE A BAD IDEA

Nick heard a quiet *click-click, click-click*. His first thought was that some animal was trying to get into the tent. Then he realized it was coming from inside. "What's that sound?" he asked.

"I'm knitting," Carter whispered, holding up his needles and ball of yarn. "That doctor dude freaked me out and I can't fall asleep." The three boys lay stretched out on their cots. A sleeping bag was folded beneath each of their beds, but even with the sun down, it was still too hot to consider climbing into one.

"He reminded me of an evil wizard, with that beard and those beady I'm-about-to-turn-you-into-a-newt eyes," Nick said. He was just able to make out the silhouettes of his friends in the dark tent. "What do you think he meant by 'a place of power'?"

Angelo sat up and put on his shoes. "That is a very good question."

"Where are you going?" Nick asked.

"Out." Angelo took a package of testing swabs from under his bed.

Nick glanced toward the flimsy curtain that divided the boys' half of the tent from his parents'. "What if my mom and dad see you?"

"Your dad is snoring like a lawn mower. If your mom is awake, I'll say I have to go to the bathroom."

"Sure, that'll work," Nick said sarcastically. "Then you can explain how you always take your swabs to the toilet with you."

Angelo held up his fingers one at a time. "One, we know that the first party who came here disappeared without a trace—exactly the way they would have if aliens abducted them. Two, we know that the pyramids are aligned to the stars. Coincidence? Three, the government was obviously hiding something by keeping people away from here for fifty years. And finally, they let a group come back that is looking for something powerful. What does that say to you?"

"The Ark of the Covenant," Carter said. "Like in

Raiders of the Lost Ark."

Nick smiled. "How would the Ark of the Covenant end up in *Mexico*?"

"German spies," Carter said at once. "Everyone knows Hitler was looking for the Ark. What better place to hide it than a pyramid in Mexico?"

Angelo didn't bother responding.

Nick put a hand on Angelo's shoulder. "Even if there *is* alien DNA here, why not look for it tomorrow, when it's light? Dr. Canul said not to go outside. Do you really want to start out this vacation by getting busted for breaking rules?"

"I gotta side with Nick," Carter said. "I'm not so big on the idea of running into an alien in the dark. Not to mention snakes, giant hairy spiders, and things with claws and teeth."

Angelo jerked away from Nick's hand. "You two can stay, but I'm going." He turned and walked out of the tent.

"What's with him?" Nick asked. "It's like he's obsessed or something." He sighed. They'd probably all get eaten. "I can't let him go alone," he said, pulling on his shoes.

Carter grabbed his yarn and jumped off the bed. "I'm not letting you two get all the credit for discovering aliens without me."

Nick was sure his mom would hear them and wake up, but he and Carter managed to tiptoe out of the tent without being noticed.

"What now?" Carter asked, eyeing the shadowy camp.

In the daylight, the tents and equipment had looked sort of like a scout troop setting up to roast hot dogs and marshmallows. But in the dim light of the moon and stars, the camp looked dark and more than a little creepy. The rain forest was so close he could throw a rock into the trees without even trying hard. Anything could be watching them from their hidden depths. The chirping and buzzing was even louder than it had been during the day. But now it sounded like the birds, frogs, and insects were warning the boys to get away while they could.

"Over there," Nick said, pointing to the shadowy figure of Angelo heading toward the pyramid of the sun.

Nick jogged toward the imposing mound, which was shrouded in swirling mist turned ghostly silver by the moonlight. He could imagine all too well people being dragged up those steps to be sacrificed for some grisly ritual.

He and Carter caught up with Angelo just as he was beginning to climb. "I told you guys you didn't have to come with me," Angelo muttered.

"Sure. Then I'd have to explain to your mom how we let you get eaten by a snake," Carter said. "Yes, ma'am, I saw him getting turned into a boa constrictor's midnight snack. His last words were something about the theory of relativity, I think."

"Very funny," Angelo said. There was definitely something wrong with him. He could be intense at times, but in all the years they'd been friends, Nick had never seen him act like this.

Nick grabbed him by the backpack and spun him around. "Not another step until you tell us what's going on."

Angelo tried to pull away. "I told you. I'm looking for DNA."

Nick refused to let go. "I've faced zombies with you. We've hunted a mad scientist. Shoot, we were nearly killed by our own evil twins together. I've seen you go through a lot of things. But I've never seen you act like a jerk to your best friends. I get that you want to find aliens. But something is different about this."

"I wouldn't say he's *never* been a jerk," Carter said. "But never one *this* big. Either you tell us what's going on or I'm waking up the whole camp."

Angelo looked at the two of them, gulped, and dropped to the ground. He wrapped his arms around his knees and buried his face in them. His back began to shake.

Nick looked down at his friend, unable to believe what he was seeing.

"Is he crying?" Carter whispered.

Nick sat next to Angelo and wrapped an arm around his friend's shoulders. "Dude, what is it? What's wrong? Whatever it is, you know we'll do anything to help."

Angelo took several hitching breaths before sobbing, "They don't want me to hunt monsters anymore."

What was he talking about? All three boys loved monsters, but they were Angelo's life. He'd been tracking monsters and keeping notes on them for as long as Nick could remember. "*Who* doesn't?"

Angelo's body shook again and he wiped his nose on the back of his arm. "My parents," he managed to gasp at last.

"What?" Carter sat on the other side of Angelo and put an arm around him too.

For the next few minutes the boys sat silently waiting for Angelo to pull himself together. Nick was sure he must have misunderstood. His parents thought his obsession with monsters was silly, and his mom thought he and his friends spent too much time watching scary movies. But they had never suggested that

69

he give up monsters completely.

After a while Angelo raised his head, took off his glasses, and wiped his eyes. "Sorry about that. It's just the thought of giving up monster hunting with you guys . . ." He brushed his hair out of his eyes. "I probably sounded like a total baby."

Carter gave Angelo a pat on the arm. "Dude, if my parents made me stop hanging out with the Monsterteers, I'd bawl like a two-year-old. I'd probably poop my pants like a two-year-old at the same time."

"How can they do that?" Nick asked. "Monsters are everything to you. What kind of jerks would make you stop doing what you love?"

"It's not like that," Angelo said. "They're trying to help me. You know how I've always wanted to be a scientist?"

Nick nodded. "Of course. With your brain, you'll probably be the next Einstein or Marie Curie, except, you know, if she was a guy."

Angelo put his glasses back on. "They know I'm smart enough, and I definitely have the grades."

"A-plus-pluses," Carter said.

"But, the thing is, they're both scientists too, and they know how important your reputation can be. They think it could hurt my chances of getting the right position when I'm older if I keep insisting monsters and aliens are real."

"Um, hello." Carter knocked on Angelo's forehead. "Monsters *are* real. We've seen them ourselves."

"*We* have. But *they* haven't."

It took Nick a second to understand what Angelo was saying. Although they'd come across zombies, living beings stitched together out of dead body parts, and much more, none of their parents had ever seen them. "They think it's all make-believe."

Angelo nodded miserably. "I want to be a scientist more than anything. But I also want to hunt for aliens. So I thought if I could just find some proof that aliens are real on this trip, maybe get their DNA . . ."

"You wouldn't have to give it up." Nick squeezed his friend's shoulder. "Why didn't you tell us earlier?"

Angelo exhaled. "I guess I was afraid you wouldn't understand. I know you love monsters as much as I do. But for you two it's more like a hobby. I want to make monsters my career. That's why I've always kept the notebook. I had this dream that one day it could be a new branch of science."

"Monsterology," Nick said. "I could totally see that."

Carter stood and grabbed Angelo's hand to pull him

up. "What are we waiting for then? Let's go find some monster skin."

"Are you serious?" Angelo said. "You'll come with me?"

Carter snorted. "Dude, we will bring E.T.'s head back in a bottle if that's what it takes."

Nick took Angelo's other hand and together the boys pulled him to his feet. "Monsterteers don't let other Monsterteers stop doing what they love. Did you remember to bring a flashlight?"

Angelo patted his belt, where not one but two thin silver flashlights were tucked. "Don't worry. I'm prepared."

"Good." Carter wiped his damp palms on the legs of his pants. "Because I want to help you find what you need. But going into a pyramid in the dark would totally freak me out."

Angelo started the steep climb up the side of the pyramid with Nick and Carter at his sides. "Why are we going up the steps?" Nick asked. "I thought we were going *inside*."

"We are," Angelo said. "The entrance is at the top."

"Say what?" Carter puffed, already a little out of breath. "I've seen tons of pyramid movies. And all of

72

them have doors in the bottom with tunnels that lead to treasure and stuff."

Angelo kept climbing, pausing only occasionally to look behind him. "You're thinking of Egyptian pyramids. Like Dr. Canul said, to the Mayans, pyramids represented mountains. They considered caves sacred passages to the underworld, so they dug them down into the mountain from the top. The passageways were often decorated with the gods and demons they expected to face after they died."

Nick felt his heart racing, and it wasn't just from the climb. "Did you say *demons*?"

"Lots of them," Angelo said, as if he was talking about math grades or what they were having for lunch. "There was Ahaltocob, the Stabbing Demon, and Ahalpuh, the Pus Demon, who caused people's bodies to swell up. Xiquiripat, the Flying Scab, and Patan, who caused people to die while coughing up blood."

Nick smiled uncertainly. "You're joking." No way was there a demon called "the Flying Scab."

Angelo rubbed his glasses on his shirt. "I'm completely serious. They all worked with the gods of death, One Death and Seven Death, setting traps and tests for people to pass on the way to the underworld. From what I've read, the traps were supposed to be pretty

73

intense, like a river filled with scorpions, and a bench to sit on that was actually a burning-hot griddle. If you made it past all the tests, you got to go to the underworld called Xibalba. Most people think it translates as 'The Place of Fear.'"

Carter grabbed Angelo by the back of his shirt, nearly pulling both of them back down the side of the pyramid. "Dude, tell me you're just making this up. If you're seriously taking us down some tunnel to a river full of scorpions, I am so out of here."

For the first time, Angelo seemed to notice how Carter and Nick were reacting to his words. "I think the river of scorpions might have been an illusion." He put his glasses back on and scratched his nose. "It's all written in that book I was telling you about—the *Popol Vuh*."

"I'm confused," Nick said. "I thought we were looking for aliens. Now you're saying we're searching for something called the Place of Fear that's filled with a bunch of demons."

The three of them stopped about three-fourths of the way up the side of the pyramid. Angelo opened his pack and took out his iPad. "What if Xibalba wasn't the name of the underworld, but the aliens' home planet?"

It sounded like the kind of thing you'd hear in a

science-fiction movie. *I come from the planet Xibalba, twenty parsecs from your home planet.*

"What about the demons?" Carter asked.

"I'm getting to that. Remember that powerful device the king's aunt and uncle were guarding for him? If it was something the aliens had left here, they'd want to keep it safe too. And what better way than to tell people it was protected by a river of scorpions, a bunch of demons, and a room filled with killer bats?"

"Hang on," Carter said, his face going noticeably paler, even in the light of the moon. "You didn't say anything about killer bats."

Angelo shut off his tablet and returned it to his pack. "I forgot to mention that part. Oh, and by the way, don't freak out, but the Mayans also viewed the entrances to the caves as the mouths of monsters. So the carvings around the doorway might be a little . . . scary."

CHAPTER 9

¿NO TE DIJE?
DIDN'T I TELL YOU?

By the time they reached the top of the pyramid, the mist seemed to be getting thicker. The sky, which had been clear when they started, was beginning to cloud up, making the night even darker than it had been.

Nick glanced down at the tents, which from this height were barely recognizable as anything more than dark shapes. "Just out of curiosity, have you ever considered the possibility that instead of making up these demons, the aliens might actually be the demons themselves?"

Angelo scratched his head. "UFO researchers have long considered the possibility that what people mistook for angels were actually extraterrestrials. I guess it only makes sense that they might be what we call demons, too."

Carter shuddered. "*Soooo*, you're saying we're going inside a cave shaped like the mouth of a monster to find aliens that may or may not cause people to die by swelling up or bleeding to death?"

The sweat that had been running down the middle of Nick's back felt ice-cold.

"It's not like they're still inside," Angelo said. "We're looking for microscopic bits of hair or skin with alien DNA on them."

Carter folded his arms across his chest, knitting needles clenched in one tightly closed fist. "And these bits of hair and skin are what made the people who went inside fifty years ago disappear without a trace?"

Angelo had no answer for that.

"I get that you want to be a famous scientist someday," Carter said. "And I totally have your back. But getting eaten by extraterrestrial demons is *not* my idea of a fun vacation."

Before Angelo could respond, Nick spotted something on the other side of the pyramid. "What's that?" he asked, pointing.

Carter and Angelo looked up. "What?" Carter asked. "I don't see anything."

Nick squinted, trying to see through the thickening mist. "It looked like some kind of light."

"Probably just the moon," Angelo said. "Or maybe a star."

"I don't think so." Nick frowned. "It looked more like a—"

The light came again. This time it was clearly a flashlight of some kind.

"There's another one," Carter said, pointing to a bobbing light a little to the right of the one Nick had seen. "Somebody's up here, walking around."

"Stay low and be quiet," Angelo said, ducking behind the altar. "We don't want them to know we're here."

"*Them?*" Carter whispered to Nick.

Nick could only shake his head. He had no idea who, or what, was on the pyramid with them, and he wasn't sure he wanted to know. But Angelo already had his tablet out and was using it to take pictures.

"Is it aliens?" Carter asked, dropping beside him. "Do they look like flying scabs?"

"Shush," Angelo hissed.

Damp with sweat and fog, Nick peeked over the edge of the cool stone. It was tough to make anything out through the swirling haze, but the beam from one of the flashlights lifted from the ground, briefly illuminating a line of men carrying boxes from the stone temple at the center of the pyramid toward the back of the platform.

"They're taking things down the back steps so they can't be spotted from the camp."

"Thieves?" Nick asked. If these men were stealing, they might be armed. In which case the boys should go back down and wake everyone up right away.

"I don't think so," Angelo said. "I recognize several of the archaeologists from the camp."

Nick rubbed the moisture from his face. "What's the point of this, then? They're allowed to take stuff from the pyramid. It's why they're here."

"I don't think they're *stealing* anything," Angelo said. "I think they're hiding it."

Carter's fingers moved nervously as he knitted one loop after another. "What would they be hiding? And who would they be hiding it from?"

"They're hiding it from *us*. So we won't see whatever they've found." Angelo got to his feet. "And I'm going to find out what they're hiding."

"Whoa, whoa, whoa." Nick jumped up and grabbed Angelo's arm. "Are you crazy? If those guys really *are* hiding something from us, what do you think they'll do if they discover we've seen them?"

"They won't. Look, the lights are gone. They're heading down the far side."

79

At the moment, everything was dark, but that didn't mean there weren't more men inside the temple, or that they wouldn't be back any minute.

"It'll take them close to an hour to carry the boxes off the pyramid and get back," Angelo said, walking toward the temple.

Nick hurried to catch up. "What are you going to do if there's someone still inside?"

"I'll figure it out when I get there." At the entrance to the temple, Angelo stared into the darkness, before pulling one of his flashlights from his belt and turning it on.

Cupping the light with the palm of his hand, Angelo stepped through the stone archway. Nick couldn't help noticing the carvings of strange, horned beasts, fanged snakes, and humans in all manner of pain.

"Reminds me of going to the dentist's office," Carter said, studying a particularly gruesome image of a man screaming.

The three boys moved quickly through the dark building. The flashlight's beam revealed stone benches, intricately patterned floors, and strange carvings on the walls. One room was empty except for six curved stones sticking out of the floor and a pair of circular holes close to the ceiling.

"What do you think those men were carrying out?" Nick asked.

"Gold," Carter said. "And jewels. Crowns and necklaces and coins, like in that movie where the kids look for the pirate treasure."

"*Goonies*," Nick said, remembering the boatload of riches all too well. One of those gold necklaces would buy every game system and video game imaginable. Not to mention every monster movie, and the materials to build some amazing Halloween costumes.

"No way." Angelo broke up their dream. "If it was treasure, why would they go to all the trouble to sneak it out? Jiménez must have told Dr. Canul what I said about aliens, and now he's trying to remove the evidence. I think it's a huge government conspiracy."

They turned a corner and Nick realized they'd gone completely through the temple. "Where's the entrance to the pyramid?"

"Maybe there *is* no entrance," Carter said. "Maybe the workers were just carrying down their equipment for the night."

That would be a relief. If there was no secret entrance, the boys could go back to the tent before they got caught, or shot, or eaten.

"Maybe," Angelo murmured. He turned around and

walked back through the temple, knocking on walls and touching carvings.

Nick noticed Carter had started knitting again. "What are you making, anyway?"

Carter held up a rectangle striped with different colors of yarn. There was a hole in the middle. He stuck his head through the hole, and the front of the rectangle barely reached his chest. "It's one of those Mexican poncho things."

"A serape," Nick said. It was ragged looking and lumpy in places, and it looked like it would take weeks, if not months, to finish. But the fact that he'd made it himself was pretty cool. "Maybe my mom could show me how to do that."

"I don't know. It's a lot harder than it looks. It makes *Dark Souls II* look like finger painting." Carter pulled off the serape and went back to work with his needles. "When it's done, I'm going to make a big hat to go with it."

A heavy grating sound came from inside the temple. Nick and Carter spun around.

"Angelo?" Nick called.

There was no answer. Nick stepped farther into the temple and called again. The building wasn't that big. Angelo should have been able to hear him from anywhere inside.

Without a light, it was hard to see anything. The boys shuffled slowly forward. Nick held a hand out in front of him to keep from running into anything.

"This is how it happens," Carter whispered from the darkness. "One minute there are three of you. The next minute there are two. Then one. The next thing you know they're making a TV movie about how you all disappeared without a trace."

"We're going to find Angelo," Nick said. But his heart was pounding. What if one of the archaeologists grabbed him? Or an alien? Or the pus demon?

Something moved behind them. Nick turned. Glowing orange eyes stared down at him. Fire shown from diamond-shaped nostrils. Sharp teeth as big as his arm glittered. It was a demon with a head as large as the room. The demon opened its huge, gaping mouth, and Nick screamed.

Carter held out his knitting needles, hands shaking. "Touch me and die!" he shouted in a quivering voice.

"*Touch me and die*?" Angelo stepped out of the demon's mouth, a wide grin on his face. "What are you going to do, knit me to death?"

As Angelo emerged from the opening, the demon's eyes and nose stopped glowing, and Nick realized the teeth were the curved stones he'd seen earlier. "It's a door," he said, his voice weak and still a little shaky.

"I told you the entrance might look like a monster," Angelo said. "Look, it's pretty cool." He pushed on one of the teeth in the floor and a stone swung down, blending in with the wall. Angelo pushed the tooth again and shoved the door open, making the grinding sound Nick and Carter had heard earlier.

"Couldn't you just have said, 'Look, guys, I found a door'?" Carter asked, lowering his needles. "You had to scare us half to death?"

Angelo laughed. "Sorry. I shut the door behind me and was trying to figure out how to open it. It's pretty awesome how the light makes it look like a monster though, isn't it?" He stepped through the door and shined the light, turning the wall back into a demon.

"Yeah, *awesome*," Carter grunted.

"Let's go down and have a look around before the archaeologists come back," Angelo said.

Nick peered down the dark passage. The walls were coated with moss and the floors looked wet and slick. "Are you sure it's safe? What about those traps you were talking about?"

Angelo handed him the second flashlight. "The archaeologists went down, and they survived."

"That's what the people with Indiana Jones say, right before they get hit by poison darts," Carter said.

Nick stepped through the demon's mouth, ducking

84

his head to keep from hitting the stone. "It can't be too dangerous, can it? I mean, they wouldn't let families come here on vacation if they could get seriously hurt."

"So far, your family is the only one here," Carter said. "Maybe that should tell you something." But he followed Angelo when he walked into the tunnel.

The passage was just as damp and slippery as Nick had imagined. He took small, shuffling steps to keep from falling, and ran one hand along the wall.

Angelo stopped at a section of wall with a series of holes drilled into it and shined his light excitedly up and down. "Look at this!"

Carter pushed past Nick to get a look, then shook his head in disgust. "Yeah, these are some totally cool *holes*. Maybe next we can find a rock. Or some dust."

"These aren't just holes. They're stars. See how they form constellations?" Angelo pointed his finger from one dot to another. "That's the Big Dipper, also known as Plough. And that's Orion." He handed Nick his flashlight and swabbed a couple of the holes, carefully noting the time and date in his notebook. "It's important to write down where we took each sample. That way, when we get an alien hit, we will be able to track everywhere they went."

Nick glanced the way they'd come, wondering how long it would be before the men came back.

"Is it time?" someone asked.

"Time for what?" Nick said.

Carter looked up from his knitting. "Dinner?"

Nick snorted. "What are you talking about? We already had dinner."

"What are *you* talking about?" Carter asked, clearly irritated. "You asked me what it was time for, and I said dinner. If that's not it, I give up. What's it time for?"

"How should I know? *You're* the one who asked."

"Would you two stop arguing," Angelo said, tucking the swabs into his testing kit. "You're going to wake the dead. And there are probably at least a few of them down here."

Nick glared at Carter, wondering what the point of the argument had been, but his friend had gone back to work on his serape.

The three of them continued down the hallway, Angelo taking DNA samples every so often.

"Are you here to free me?" a voice asked.

Nick spun around, sure Carter was messing with him again, but Carter had drifted behind a little and was fiddling with his serape.

"Did you say something?" Nick asked Angelo.

Angelo barely glanced up from his work. "Nope. Why?"

Nick shrugged. "No reason, I guess I thought I

heard something." Maybe it was the strange carvings on the walls, or maybe it was the fact that they were going deeper and deeper down a pathway that supposedly led to the underworld, but he was starting to feel a little freaked out.

The deeper they went into the pyramid, the cooler the air got and the narrower the passage grew. Soon, Angelo had to duck to keep from hitting his head. Nick tried to imagine what it would be like to be shut up in this cold, small tunnel, and he shivered.

At the top of a staircase, Nick noticed a carving of a man in a small boat floating down a river. The man was wearing a feathered crown and a fur that might have been the pelt of a jaguar. "What's that all about?" he whispered, running his finger along the curving lines of the river.

"The river of the dead," a voice whispered back.

This time both Carter and Angelo were too far away to have said what he'd just heard. "That's it," he said, backing away from the wall. "I'm getting out of here."

Angelo, who had been kneeling a little farther up the tunnel, put away his swab and walked over. "What's wrong?"

"I thought I heard something," Nick said, the skin on his arms breaking out in goose bumps. "A kind of whispering."

Carter joined them and tilted his head. "I hear something too."

"You do?" Nick asked. Maybe he wasn't going crazy after all.

Angelo nodded. "It's coming from down there. A kind of *shhhhh* sound."

The three of them looked down the staircase.

"I'm officially freaked out," Carter said.

Angelo started down the stairs, but both Nick and Carter grabbed him.

"Are you crazy?" Nick asked. "There could be anything down there."

"Which is why we have to find out," Angelo said. "I want to find the room those men were bringing the boxes from. That might be our best chance to find alien traces."

Nick rubbed his lips. The voices had totally freaked him out, and all he wanted to do was go back into the tent.

"You can wait here," Angelo said. "I'll take a quick look and come right back."

"No," Carter said at once. "As soon as we split up, the mummies will come and rip out our eyeballs."

Nick crossed his arms in front of his chest, hands cupping his elbows. "Thanks for those encouraging

88

words." But Angelo was right. They had to find out what was going on now, or they might never get another chance. "Okay, we go down. But only to the bottom of the stairs. Then we're out of here."

Carter and Angelo nodded.

Walking single file, they started down the staircase. The steps were treacherous, worn smooth and slippery by who knew how many footsteps. Angelo led the way—flashlight probing the darkness ahead of him. Carter came next, and Nick was in the back, constantly checking over his shoulder.

The farther down the staircase they went, the louder the whispering became. Nick began to imagine what awaited them at the bottom of the steps. Poisonous snakes, giant scorpions, three-headed aliens, mummies with bandages trailing behind them. Each image was worse than the last.

Carter must have been having the same thoughts, because he held his serape out to Nick. "If I don't make it, I want you to have this."

"We're all going to make it," Angelo said. "Look, we've reached the bottom of the—"

Before he could complete his sentence, something reached out of the darkness and grabbed him.

CHAPTER 10

NUNCA,
JAMÁS MIENTAS
A TUS PADRES

NEVER,
EVER LIE TO
YOUR PARENTS

Angelo yelped and dropped his bag of swabs. Carter wheeled around and ran straight into Nick, covering him in loose yarn and knocking the flashlight out of his hands. Wrapped in Carter's yarn, like a fly in a spider-web, Nick could only watch in terror as the dark figure turned Angelo around.

"What are you boys doing down here?" a stern voice asked.

"Dr. Canul," Nick said, a wave of relief washing over him. A bright light shined in his eyes, almost completely blinding him.

"I told you three to stay in your tents."

"We, um, had to go to the bathroom," Carter said,

trying to untangle the yarn from himself and Nick.

"The *bathroom*? At this time of night?" Dr. Canul's dark eyes glared at each of the boys. "And you chose to do it inside one of the greatest archaeological digs of this century?"

Nick felt something sharp jabbing him in the back, and retrieved one of Carter's knitting needles. "Well, we didn't exactly *go* to the bathroom. We were going to, but . . ."

"We saw flashlights," Angelo jumped in. "And we were afraid thieves were breaking into the pyramid. And look who we found. Maybe you can explain what *you're* doing down here at this time of night."

The doctor's thin lips pressed so tightly together that they looked sharp enough to slice cheese. "I have no need to answer to a bunch of trespassing children. But if you must know, my men discovered a new cache of valuable pieces just after dinner. I wanted to get them safely stored and cataloged before morning."

"Pieces?" Angelo asked. "Are you sure you don't mean *alien artifacts*?"

"Aliens?" Dr. Canul sputtered. "Is that what this is about? Please tell me you're not one of those crazies." He rolled his eyes. "*Take me to your leader.*"

Angelo dropped his head. Nick couldn't help feeling sorry for his friend.

"What are these?" Dr. Canul asked, picking up the bag of swabs.

Carter snatched it out of his hand. "Q-tips."

The doctor narrowed his eyes.

Carter stuck a finger into one ear and twisted it. "Jungles give me nasty earwax. I could start a candle factory."

Dr. Canul puffed out his cheeks and exhaled loudly.

"There's something down here," Nick said, pointing past the archaeologist. "I heard it whispering."

Dr. Canul rolled his eyes. "Did you really?" He waggled his fingers in the air. "Maybe it's ghosts. *Booo. Booo.*"

"I heard it too," Carter said. "It was kind of a whooshing sound."

"We all heard it," Angelo agreed.

"Come with me." Dr. Canul marched them around the corner to a small waterfall dropping into a pool of deep blue water. "What you heard was this. You boys could easily have stumbled into it in the dark. And drowned."

The archaeologist pointed to the stairs. "This is exactly the sort of reason you shouldn't be here. And I will see to it that you do not step a foot inside this site again. You three will return to your tents, where I will wake up your parents and tell them exactly what you have done."

"That won't be necessary," Nick said, thinking of his mom's reaction. "You have things to do here, and we can tell them ourselves."

The tall, bearded man shook his head and marched them up the stairs.

Nick gulped. This wasn't going to be pretty.

"I can't believe you did something like that," Mom growled. It was seven o'clock the next morning, and she was still furious. "If we were home, I'd ground you for the rest of your life. I'm tempted to leave you in the tent for the rest of the day."

Angelo opened his mouth, but Nick shook his head. He knew his parents well enough to understand that nothing he and his friends said now would make a difference. Besides, he could just imagine his parents' response to one of Angelo's rambling lectures on how the pyramid was actually the home to aliens. "It was really dumb, and we'll never do it again," Nick said.

Dad pulled his Indiana Jones hat low on his head. "You're right, you won't. The least you could have done was invited me to come with you." Mom gave him a look and he quickly backtracked. "What I meant to say was that you will not leave the tent without letting one of us know where you are at all times."

"Yes," Nick said. Some vacation this was turning out to be.

Mom gave them all a disapproving look. Even Carter, whose knitting progress had clearly blown her away, wasn't spared.

"Let's get some breakfast," Dad said. "I'm so hungry I could eat a flying monkey."

Silently the five of them trooped across the camp to the meal tent. Along the way, Nick noticed that most of the men were already at work. "Why are there no women archaeologists?" he asked.

"Maybe they're too smart to come out here," Carter said, slapping a bug on his neck.

"More likely Dr. Canul is sexist," Angelo said. "Some of the best scientists in the world are women."

Nick yawned. "Guess they start early around here."

"The early archaeologist unearths the worm," a cheerful voice said. Mr. Jiménez walked out of the meal tent with a straw hat tilted jauntily on his head and a red bandanna tied around his neck. "It's an archaeologist joke. Because we dig things up, and worms live in the ground."

When no one laughed, he lifted his hands. "I didn't say it was a *good* joke." He nodded sympathetically at the boys. "I understand you had a little run-in with the good doctor last night."

"Don't bring it up," Carter said.

"Ahh." Mr. Jiménez twined his fingers together and leaned toward Nick's parents. "Don't be too hard on them. Boys will be boys. And the doctor can be a little, shall we say, *intense* when it comes to his projects."

"It won't happen again," Mom said.

"Of course not." Mr. Jiménez grinned. "Come, let's get you fed. We have a busy day ahead."

"Are we going inside the pyramid?" Dad asked. His hand went to his belt, and Nick noticed his father's Indiana Jones whip coiled at his side.

"Not today." Mr. Jiménez led them into the tent, which was thick with the aroma of fresh tortillas and eggs. He nodded to Mom and Dad. "We will start the two of you with cleaning and sorting valuable artifacts."

"Treasure?" Dad asked, beaming.

"*Priceless* treasures," Mr. Jiménez said with a wink.

"What about us?" Nick asked as the cook filled his plate with steaming eggs.

"Do we get to look at the treasure too?" Carter asked.

Mr. Jiménez patted Carter on the head. "We have a

very special job for you boys."

All through breakfast Nick wondered what their special job would be. Maybe there were tunnels so small only kids could fit inside. Maybe the archaeologists would lower them into treasure rooms on ropes and let them pry open caskets. Maybe they'd get to look for the item of power—the missing link that could prove Angelo's theory once and for all.

But after they cleared their trays and marched out to the site, they discovered that their *special* job was none of those. Their first clue was when they were given thick gloves and pruning shears.

"What are these for?" Carter asked. "They look like the kind of cutters my dad uses in the garden."

That's exactly what they were. Dr. Canul had ordered a couple of workers to run knotted ropes down the side of the pyramid of the moon—which was much steeper and harder to scale than the pyramid of the sun. When they reached the top, they found themselves cutting vines and bushes away from the crumbling stone buildings there. Unlike at the other temple, it didn't look like anyone had bothered to come up here, and plants were growing everywhere.

"I can't believe this is our *special* job," Nick complained. It was backbreaking work snipping off the thick, woody branches, and his arms ached after less than an hour. Plus, the mosquitoes were relentless—buzzing around his face and biting every square inch of skin they could find. Meanwhile his mom and dad were sitting in the shade getting to see treasures.

"I suspect Dr. Canul had something to do with it," Angelo said. "He probably wants to keep us as far away from whatever he's up to as possible." He pulled away a long section of vine from a dangerously leaning wall and tossed it aside. "I wish I had my DNA results to prove aliens are real."

Nick waved at a cloud of mosquitoes. "Couldn't you have started the tester this morning?"

"I could if I had electricity," Angelo said. "Somehow we've got to find a way to plug into one of the camp generators."

"If I'd known I was going to be a gardener, I'd have stayed at the hotel," Carter said, although he'd cut bushes for only a few minutes before going back to his knitting. "And when we get done, we have to climb back down the pyramid again. We'll be lucky if we don't fall and break our legs."

Nick scissored his shears on the trunk of a leafy bush, straining until the blade finally cut through. "I wonder why this pyramid is so much steeper than the other one. It's almost like the people who built it didn't want anyone to climb it."

Angelo leaned against the stone wall, using its shade to cool off a little, and took a long drink from his canteen. "They probably didn't."

"What do you mean?" Nick kicked away the bush he'd cut and joined Angelo in the shade. The bugs were as bad, but it felt good to get out of the broiling sun.

"The Mayans built two kinds of pyramids," Angelo said. "One was meant to be climbed. They used those for sacrifices and other ceremonies. Did you notice how big the temple there was compared to this one? The other kind—*this* kind—was more sacred. It was climbed rarely and was usually considered the home to a powerful god."

Nick glanced at the shadowy interior of the temple behind him. Unlike the temple on the pyramid of the sun, this one looked like it could fall over with one big push. "What kind of god?"

Angelo shook his head. "No idea. The first archaeologists who came here didn't even realize there *were* two pyramids. They thought this was a hill." He brushed away the vines hanging over the entrance and walked inside.

Nick paused outside the entrance to the temple. The ruined building had a dank, moldy sort of smell to it that made him think of open coffins and rotting bodies. Plus, the events of the night before still freaked him out a little. Had he heard the voices of ghosts, or had it really been only the sound of the underground river? Hesitantly, he followed Angelo.

It looked like no one had been inside for hundreds of years. Vines, grass, and even a few small trees grew from cracks in stone. It was like walking into a damp, hot cave. Everything was hidden in shadows, and the floors were covered with dark green plants that felt slippery beneath his feet.

"It smells like the monkey cages in the zoo," Carter said, coming in behind him. "You think there are any animals living in here?"

Nick looked around. *Great, another thing to worry about.*

Angelo brushed away dirt and vines from one of the walls, exposing faint carvings of people. "I think this is some kind of history of the kings. That's obviously the boy king. This is his father the king. Then this must be the boy king's grandfather." He shook his head. "I wish I could read these hieroglyphs; I might be able to figure out who, or what, was worshiped here."

"*Si pudieras leer jeroglíficos, perdería mi trabajo,*" said a female voice.

Nick stumbled toward the light of the doorway. "Did

99

you hear that?" he squeaked.

From behind the wall stepped a woman with long, dark hair and brown eyes that looked like bottomless pits. With her face half hidden in the shadows, Nick couldn't tell whether she was real or a ghost. But Carter and Angelo seemed to see her as well.

The woman looked the three boys over. "Do you mind . . . telling me what . . . the three of you are . . . doing here?"

Angelo held out his clippers. "We're, um, cutting vines."

"Who are you?" Nick said, getting back his nerve. "And what did you say before?"

The woman moved into the light, and her eyes, which had looked scary before, now gleamed with interest. "*Si pudieras leer jeroglíficos, perdería mi trabajo.* If you could read hieroglyphs, I'd lose my job."

"You work here?" Carter blurted. "But you're a lady."

The woman tilted her head. "*Gracias por notarla.* Thank you for noticing. And you are a . . . boy, I believe? Or possibly some sort of howler monkey? You have the voice for it."

Carter blushed. "I didn't mean . . . It's just . . . I didn't know there were any ladies working here." He looked at Nick. "I mean, besides Nick's mom."

The woman flashed the smallest bit of white teeth in what might have been a smile. "I'm Dr. Sofia Lopez. And I believe you must be Nick, Carter, and Angelo."

"How did you know our names?" Nick asked. He didn't remember seeing the woman around the camp—either when they'd arrived or at any of the meals.

"I know more than that," she said. "You might say knowing things is my job. But what I don't know is why you're here. From what I've heard, all the excitement is at *la pirámide del sol*." She jerked her thumb toward the other pyramid.

Nick clipped a vine and pulled it viciously from the wall. "We got caught trying to explore last night."

"Dr. Canul was none too happy about it," Angelo said.

Dr. Lopez nodded knowingly. "That explains it, all right. You've been exiled to the *boring* pyramid."

"You could say that," Nick said.

Carter stuck his needles into his yarn ball. "Are you an archaeologist?"

Nick thought it was kind of a dumb question. After all, who else would be climbing around a crumbling pyramid? But the woman shook her head. "As a matter of fact, I'm not. I'm a librarian."

101

CHAPTER 11

QUÉ MUJER TAN ENCANTADORA

WHAT A CHARMING WOMAN

Carter leaned past the woman to look deeper into the temple. "Are you saying there are a bunch of books in here?"

"*Libros?*" the woman asked, clearly confused.

"You said you were a *librarian*," Carter said. "This is like the most run-down library I've ever seen."

"Ahh." She smiled. "Not that kind of librarian. I am an expert on Mayan script."

Angelo's eyes lit up.

"You know what these hiero-whatchamacallits mean?" Nick asked, pointing to the pictures carved into the walls.

"Hieroglyphs. From the Latin words *hieros*, meaning

'sacred,' and *glyphe*, meaning 'carving.'" Dr. Lopez ran a finger gently over the dirt-crusted wall, and Angelo stared at her like he was in love. "That's actually a mistake though. Early European explorers thought these carvings looked like Egyptian hieroglyphs."

"But Mayan writing is no more related to the Egyptian hieroglyphs than English is to Japanese," Angelo said.

"Correct." Dr. Lopez smiled, making Angelo beam. "Mayan script is composed of five hundred and fifty logograms, which represent whole words, and a hundred and fifty syllabograms, which represent—"

"Syllables," Angelo cut in. "I got that far in my reading. But I never made it to the actual translations."

Nick could see the two of them going on all day like this, and his stomach was already starting to growl for lunch. "Could we, um, get to the point? If you can read this script stuff, what does it say?" He gave Angelo a meaningful look. "And how does it help us figure out whether you-know-whats were you-know-where?"

Angelo frowned.

Dr. Lopez looked from one boy to the other. It was obvious she wanted an explanation, but Nick wasn't sure he wanted to tell her anything. The last two times they'd brought up aliens, it hadn't gone very well.

Apparently Angelo felt the same way. He quickly turned the conversation back to the carvings. "What does this say? It looks like a history of the kings."

The librarian gave Nick one last curious glance before turning to study the wall. She cleared away dirt and pulled down several vines. "Yes." She traced her finger along a series of carvings that made no sense at all to Nick. Occasionally she would brush at the wall, trying to make something out.

"The Mayans believed in three planes: the earth; the underworld, Xibalba, below; and the heavens above. They believed that the sun and the moon were gods who left the sky every night and went to the underworld. Thus, this pyramid was for the goddess of the moon, and the other pyramid honored the god of the sun. The Mayans believed that when you die you must pass through the underworld—a place of tests and trials. Caves, tunnels, and sacred pools were believed to be entrances to Xibalba."

"See. That's what I was telling you about," Angelo said.

She pointed to the text Angelo had been unable to figure out. "According to this, male royalty were buried in the pyramid of the sun. The boy king, his father, and his grandfather. Female royalty were buried here.

His mother was not considered to have royal blood, because she married into the line." She touched a picture of a woman in a fancy headdress. "But the king's father had one sibling—a sister. She was the boy's aunt and would have been royalty. If those of royal blood passed through Xibalba, they could be reborn as gods in the sky."

Angelo leaned forward, his eyes gleaming. "They thought their kings went to the *sky*?"

Dr. Lopez nodded. "If they passed certain tests. The carvings in this temple are interesting. If I'm reading them right, they seem to be talking about an item of power that belonged to the king. The item," she said, pointing to another picture that looked like a chest, "was being held for the king by his aunt and uncle. I think it was to help him get past the death gods, One Death and Seven Death."

She pulled away more vines. "Hmmm. This is a little worn away. I'll have to bring back my equipment and see if I can clear it up. But I think the item was somehow associated with the ten demons of death."

Nick felt a cold chill run over his body. All this talk of demons and death was freaking him out. Especially in this small, foul-smelling building. But Angelo walked deeper inside, eyes wide, like he'd just been given a free pass to Disneyland. He stopped beside a crumbling slab. "Is this another altar?"

The librarian nodded. "As you can see, it's quite heavily damaged. The entire temple is in bad shape. It's one of the reasons the archaeologists have spent most of their time exploring the other pyramid instead of this one. I'd take you inside, but I'm afraid you'd find it rather boring."

Carter looked up from his nearly finished serape. "Are you saying we can go in?"

Dr. Lopez waved a cloud of mosquitoes from her face. "There's not much to see. But it would get us away from the bugs."

"Show me the way," Angelo said, bouncing on the balls of his feet.

The librarian smiled. "You're practically standing on it." She herded the boys back from the altar and knelt on the one completely clear section of floor. The floor was covered with a series of carvings that seemed to represent the day and night skies. "The trigger is *muy ingenioso*. You place one hand on the moon, one hand on the sun, push down on both, and . . ."

There was an audible *click*, and the altar moved ever so slightly. Dr. Lopez stood up and pushed the altar. It turned with a low rumble, revealing a dark staircase.

106

Cool, musty air rose from the opening.

"Awesome," Carter said. "Are there any coffins or treasure?"

Dr. Lopez waved a hand. "See for yourself."

"I wish I'd brought my swabs," Angelo said.

"Your what?" The librarian frowned.

Angelo blinked. "I mean, my um, flashlight."

"You won't need it." Dr. Lopez walked down the stairs, her body slowly disappearing as she moved farther into the entrance. "As you can see, the people who built the pyramid thought of everything." Her voice echoed from below.

Angelo hurried down the stairs behind her. "You guys have to see this," he called up.

Carter tucked his knitting under one arm and started down the steps. "You coming?"

Nick rubbed his hands on his dusty jeans. "Maybe I'll just wait out here."

"Afraid a mummy will grab you?" Carter grinned. "The great thing about mummies is they're really slow. You could *walk* away from them and still not get caught. Unless they have motorcycles. I saw this one movie where these mummies were all riding Harleys. Every once in a while one of them would get his bandages caught in the—"

107

"Fine," Nick interrupted. "I'll come down if you promise to stop talking."

"*Excuse me*," Carter said, disappearing into the dark entrance. "Some people *like* a good mummy movie."

"Some people know the difference between a *good* mummy movie and a *bad* one." Nick took one last look around the temple and headed down the stairs.

The first thing he noticed when he reached the bottom of the staircase was that although they were underground, the tunnel was nearly as light as the temple. "Torches?" he asked, looking around.

"Better," Angelo said. He pointed to a series of polished metal dishes that looked sort of like brass. "They made mirrors to reflect the sun from the entrance."

"Not quite," Dr. Lopez said. "Both of the pyramids of Aktun are built to mark the summer solstice—the longest day of the year—and the winter solstice—the shortest day of the year."

She tapped the closest mirror to the entrance. "I've been polishing these mirrors and studying how they align on different dates. My guess is that at a certain point during the winter solstice, the moon reflects through the temple roof, down the stairs, and off one mirror to another all the way to the bottom of this pyramid. Tomorrow night is the winter solstice, and I was hoping to check it." The librarian sighed. "Unfortunately that isn't going to happen."

"Why not?" Nick asked, interested in spite of his nervousness.

"Look for yourself." Dr. Lopez pointed down the tunnel.

The boys turned to see that the sloping hallway ended abruptly after less than a dozen feet.

"That's it?" Carter asked, walking to the dead end. "What a rip-off. What did they do, forget to pay their workers?"

"I wish I knew," Dr. Lopez said. "That's what I've been trying to figure out since I got here. Dr. Canul thinks this was simply a place to store items used during ceremonies in the temple. Maybe he's right."

Angelo studied the wall at the end of the tunnel. "There's something carved here."

The librarian nodded. "Good eye. I didn't spot it myself right away. The writing is faint. It's not as easy to make out as some of the temple writings. But from what I can tell, there seem to be two possible translations. The first is simply 'This is the start.'"

"The start of what?" Angelo asked. "It should say, 'This is the end.'"

Carter laughed. "That's awesome. It's like a Mayan

knock-knock joke. Knock knock. Who's there? No one. This isn't even a door."

Nick shook his head. "I'm pretty sure the Mayans weren't into knock-knock jokes."

Dr. Lopez raised her hands. "Maybe it *is* a joke. I've searched every inch of this passage and there is no way to get past that wall."

"What's the other translation?" Nick asked.

"*Death is the start*," Dr. Lopez said in a soft voice that didn't sound at all like her.

Nick turned around. "'Death is the start'? What does that even mean?"

The librarian gaped at him, eyes wide. "How did you know that?"

"Know what?" Nick asked.

"It's taken me over a week to figure out that translation. And even then I wasn't sure. How did you translate that?"

"I didn't translate anything. You told me what it said." Nick realized Carter and Angelo were staring at him. "You guys heard Dr. Lopez? I asked her what the second translation was, and she said, 'Death is the start.'"

Both his friends shook their heads.

"*Death is the start. And the time is close at hand,*"

said the same voice that had spoken before. Only this time, Nick could see Dr. Lopez's lips weren't moving. Suddenly the room seemed too tight around him. The cold air felt like a finger running down his back, and he couldn't breathe. "I have to get out of here now," he gasped.

CHAPTER 12

¿EN EL PRINCIPIO DE QUÉ?

THE BEGINNING OF WHAT?

"Are you going to tell us what happened back there?" Angelo asked.

The three boys were in the meal tent, huddled together at a table over lunch. Despite his friends' questions and the librarian's curiosity, he'd refused to talk about what he'd heard inside the pyramid. All he'd wanted to do was get out of there and back to camp.

Nick took a bite of his refried beans and stared at his plate. "I told you. Nothing happened."

Angelo folded his arms. "How did you know what the carvings said?"

"It made sense. Think about it. Like a dead end. This is the beginning. Death is the beginning."

"You're saying you *guessed*?" Carter asked around a mouthful of tortilla.

"Sure." Nick knew neither of his friends was buying his story. He wouldn't have in their place. But he wasn't about to tell them he was hearing voices again.

Fortunately, he didn't have to answer any more of their questions, because at that moment his mom and dad walked into the tent.

"How was your morning?" Mom asked, getting in line for lunch. "Your dad and I have been having a ball. We got to handle items that haven't been touched by human hands for hundreds, if not thousands, of years."

Nick scowled. "Glad to see you missed me."

Mom stopped with a food tray in her hands. "What's that supposed to mean?"

Nick only grunted, but Carter gave him a funny look.

Dad took off his hat and wiped his forehead with the back of his arm as though he'd just returned from hiking through the jungle. He took a plate and sat at the table beside the boys. "It was like being Indiana Jones. Can you imagine how it feels to hold in your hands treasures most men only dream of?"

"No," Nick said grumpily. "I can't. I spent the day

cutting bushes. I felt more like Gardener Bob than Indiana Jones."

"It's your own fault," Mom said, brushing off a bench before taking a seat. "If you hadn't snuck out last night, you could be sorting artifacts too."

"Thanks for reminding me," Nick said. He was done with his lunch, but the last thing he wanted to do was climb back up the pyramid and chop more vines.

He noticed Angelo looking outside the tent and realized his friend was staring at one of the industrial generators outside. He leaned close enough to whisper, "You aren't thinking of plugging into that, are you?"

"I need to check the DNA before Dr. Canul realizes I have it," Angelo whispered back.

"How are you going to use their electricity without them noticing?"

Angelo smiled. "I have a plan."

"This is your plan?" Nick asked as the three boys stood outside the supply tent where all the camp's equipment was stored. "You're just going to walk in there and ask for an extension cord? You might as well walk straight up to Dr. Canul and say, 'Hey, I'm going to test my DNA samples now.'"

Angelo looked around to make sure none of the

archaeologists were watching. "Just keep an eye out."

Nick knew that Angelo was anxious to prove there had been aliens in the pyramids. But he also knew they were already in trouble for sneaking out the night before. One more slipup and they'd probably get sent home and Nick would be grounded for the rest of his life. "Couldn't you wait to test the swabs until we get back to civilization?"

"If I wait until we're gone to find out that I didn't get any samples of alien DNA, it'll be too late to look for more. Once we have proof of the aliens, we can confront Dr. Canul and force him to tell us the truth. Then my mom and dad will have to let me keep studying monsters and aliens."

"Yeah, I see confronting Dr. Canul going *really* well." Carter snorted. He and Angelo stared at each other. Carter hated it when Angelo acted like he knew everything, and meanwhile Angelo wouldn't listen to reason when he thought he was on the verge of a big discovery.

"Fine," Nick said. "But make it quick."

Angelo took one last look around, brushed as much of the dirt off his pants and shirt as he could, and approached the man just inside the tent. "¡Hola!"

The man looked up from the tools he was cleaning. Angelo pointed to something inside the tent.

"Necesito un cable de extension."

The man raised his hands and said something back in Spanish. Nick didn't bother trying to understand the conversation. He eased up to the side of the tent and peeked around the corner, feeling like the driver at a bank robbery. He was sure that any minute someone in authority would show up and ask why they weren't on the pyramid cutting bushes.

"You know what I don't get?" Carter said, making Nick jump.

"Geez, don't do that," Nick yelped. "You scared the snot out of me."

Carter didn't seem overly concerned. His knitting needles clicked together with a machinelike consistency. "What I don't get is why Dr. Canul invited us here in the first place."

"Huh?"

"Well, clearly he's not happy we're here. I mean, did you hear him last night at dinner? It's like we were a bunch of tourists trampling all over his precious pyramid."

Nick thought about that for a second. "Technically, we kind of are. I mean, Angelo knows a lot about pyramids and stuff, but we're not archaeologists. For us, this is a vacation. For them, it's their job."

116

"Right. So why invite us in the first place? If this place is so sacred that no outsiders have ever been allowed on the site, why let two parents and a bunch of kids stick their noses in everything?"

Nick stared at his friend. It was easy to take Carter for granted. Usually he was cracking jokes or begging for food. And with all his knitting, Nick had assumed Carter wasn't even listening to what was going on around him. Then he came up with something like this. "That's a great question. Why *did* he let us come? I mean, all he had to do was tell the people booking the vacation this was a closed site. It's kind of weird."

Carter raised an eyebrow. "*Very* weird."

Nick looked out at the camp, and another thought occurred to him. "You know what else is weird? That we're the only tourists here. What kind of archaeology group opens their site up to people on vacation but invites only one family?"

"I got it," Angelo said, hurrying from the supply tent. For a minute, Nick thought Angelo was saying he had an answer to Carter's question. Then he saw the bright orange cord looped around his friend's arm. "Now we just have to plug it into a generator, run it back to our tent, and prove aliens exist."

Although Nick had his doubts, it was actually a lot

easier than he expected. Angelo walked up to one of the camp's generators like he knew what he was doing. He studied the connections for a moment, then plugged in the end of the cord and unreeled it back to their tent. Although several men walked by, none of them so much as glanced in the boys' direction.

Once they were safely out of sight in the tent, Nick felt a little less stressed. "I'm surprised the archaeologists didn't check for DNA themselves," he said as Angelo plugged in the tester and began making adjustments.

Angelo put one of the swabs he'd taken last night into a test tube and shook it. He inserted the tube into the machine, pushed a button, and grabbed another swab. "They probably did. If I'm right, they've known for years that aliens built the pyramids. They've just been hiding it from the rest of the world."

Carter laughed. "Why would they do that? If people knew aliens built the pyramids, they would all pay big bucks to come and see them."

"He has a point," Nick said. "I'll bet the pyramids would be, like, bigger than Disneyland."

Now it was Angelo's turn to laugh. "Why does our government keep the alien spacecraft in that mysterious military base called Area 51 a secret? Why do my parents insist there's no such thing as Bigfoot or the

Loch Ness Monster? Because if we all admitted monsters were real, people would freak out. There'd be panic. No one would be able to sleep at night knowing they might be beamed up at any minute."

Nick could believe that. If his parents knew that he, Angelo, and Carter had met zombies, creatures sewn together from spare body parts, and their own evil doppelgängers, they wouldn't let them out of the house until they were thirty. "You think they're throwing away the evidence then?"

"Nope," Angelo said, putting another tube in the tester. "The whole reason governments keep places like Area 51 is to try to figure out how the aliens' technology worked. None of the countries talk about what they're doing, because they're all competing to build their own flying saucer first."

He pushed a couple of more buttons and watched something on the screen. "Plus, you saw how proud Dr. Canul was of being a direct descendant of the people who built the pyramids. Can you imagine his reaction if he had to admit the Mayans didn't build them at all? The same thing goes for the Egyptians, the Chinese. Every country that's been taking credit for building the pyramids would have to admit they had nothing to do with it."

Angelo put the last swab into a tube, stuck it in the

machine, and shut the cover. The tester began to whir softly and the screen filled with moving lines.

"Well?" Carter said, putting down his knitting. "What does it say? Were the pyramids made by aliens?"

Angelo studied the screen. "The full testing process could take a day or two. But we should know in a few minutes if there is any nonhuman DNA."

"Can I ask you something?" Carter said, and Nick realized after a moment that Carter was talking to him, not Angelo.

Nick shrugged. "Sure. But if it's about knitting, I'm clueless."

"I don't want to be nosy or anything. And you can tell me to mind my own business. But what's up with you and your mom?"

"What are you talking about?" Nick asked.

"You seem kind of weird around her lately."

"I don't know. It just sucks that she and my dad get to do cool stuff while we have to pick weeds." He hoped that would satisfy Carter and he would go back to his knitting, but Carter didn't accept his answer.

"No. You've been mad at her almost since the trip started. Is it because she taught me to knit? I can stop if it's bugging you."

One again, Nick was amazed by how much Carter

noticed when he didn't seem to be paying attention. He glanced toward Angelo, who was adjusting something on the tester. Had he noticed too?

Carter shook his head. "He's so gaga about the alien stuff, he wouldn't notice a venomous snake until it bit him on the butt. So spit it out. What's wrong?"

Nick sighed. "Have you ever wondered if your parents wished they'd never had you?"

"Dude, I don't have to *wonder*." Carter laughed. "Every time I leave a mess on the table or stink up the bathroom, my mom goes, 'Tell me why I had you again?'"

Nick tried to smile, but the words hit a little too close to home. Clearly Carter's mom was joking. But what if Nick's mom *really* felt that way? "I keep thinking about how my mom speaks Spanish and I never knew it. And she seems to be having such a great time here. I forget that she had a whole other life before I came along and changed all that. It's not like we have all that much in common either. I like video games, anime, and monsters. She hates all those. And I never thought to ask about what she likes."

He looked down at his hands, realized they were clenched into fists, and finger by finger forced them to uncurl. "I don't mind that she taught you to knit. In fact, it's pretty cool. But what if she wanted to teach me how to knit, or speak Spanish, or whatever else she's into, and I just never paid attention? Maybe she wishes she could take it all back and never have me in the first place. So she could keep living the life she had."

Carter stared at him. "Dude, you can't really think your mom doesn't love you."

"Of course she loves me," Nick said. "She has to. But what if she doesn't *like* me?"

The DNA tester beeped and Angelo pulled a strip of paper out of the box.

"Well?" Carter asked. "Did you find hair from E.T.'s missing toupee?"

Angelo slumped and ran his hand over his face. "No. Nothing."

CHAPTER 13

SI UNA TEORÍA NO VALE, BUSCA OTRA

IF ONE THEORY DOESN'T WORK, FIND ANOTHER

"Maybe the tests were wrong," Nick said.

Angelo sighed from his cot. They'd spent the four hours since his test cutting weeds, and he still seemed as depressed as when the results had come back negative. "The tests aren't wrong. The machine found several traces of DNA. All human."

"What if it's not working right?" Nick said. "Try it on us. We can be one of those—what do you call the people scientists use to compare to?"

"A control group." Angelo rolled off his cot. "I guess it couldn't hurt." He took out four swabs, wiping one inside Nick's mouth, another in Carter's, and a third on his hard hat. "See if you can find a hair or something of your mom's."

Nick went into the other side of the tent and came back with a strand of hair too long to be his dad's. "I found it on her brush."

Angelo put each of the swabs and hair samples into test tubes and put them in the machine. The three boys watched anxiously as the machine buzzed and whirred. Several minutes later, it beeped.

Angelo pulled out the strip of paper and shook his head. "It's working fine. See, it even knows you and your mom are related."

Carter sat on his cot, adding pockets to his serape. "Maybe you're just a lousy detective. I saw this TV show where the cop totally checked in the wrong places for DNA. His boss was like, 'That's it, dude! You're back on crosswalk duty.'"

"Stop it," Nick hissed. "You're not helping."

"What? I'm saying maybe he didn't, you know, test for DNA in the right places. There could be tons of alien DNA. You have to find out where they brushed their teeth or took a—"

"Stop." Angelo rubbed his eyes. "I guess I can try a few more swabs once this batch of testing is complete. It's just, I was so sure that if I rubbed the altar and the places you would have touched walking up and down the tunnels, I'd find at least a trace of alien DNA." He kicked his backpack. "I have to admit I might have been wrong. It's possible aliens didn't build the pyramids after all. I guess after this trip you guys will have to hunt monsters without me. You can have my notebook if you want."

Nick hated seeing Angelo so depressed. "You know," he said, "there's one thing we haven't tested."

"The outhouses?" Carter asked. "Because if I was an alien, that's totally where—"

"No," Nick said. "We're not going on a search for alien poop. I don't care how famous it would make us. The thing we haven't checked is whatever those men were carrying out of the pyramid last night."

For the first time since his results had come back negative, Angelo looked interested.

"We have no idea what was in the boxes," Carter said.

"No. But we know someone who might." Nick pulled on the shoes that he'd kicked off earlier. "My mom and dad have been indexing everything that came from the site. All we have to do is see what has shown up in the last twelve hours."

Angelo grabbed his notebook and a pack of swabs. "Great idea. Let's go."

125

Outside, the sun was beginning to set and people were finishing their work and putting things away. The rain forest was as noisy as ever, and Nick could almost imagine they were walking past cages at some tropical zoo.

"What if nothing new has shown up?" Carter asked as the boys walked through the camp.

"Then we'll know they're hiding something," Angelo said.

As soon as Nick smelled the aroma of roasted corn and grilled meat, he knew where he'd find his dad. Sure enough, as soon as he stuck his head inside the meal tent, he saw his parents. Mom was sitting at a table, reading a paperback book by the light of a sputtering gas lantern while she ate.

Dad was back in line getting a second helping of everything. Spotting the boys, he waved. "Better hurry and get some food. We working folk build up a hearty appetite."

Carter snorted. "Put him on weed patrol for a couple of hours and let him see what real work is like."

"Look who's talking." Angelo pointed at Carter's yarn. "You spent most of your time knitting."

"Hey," Carter said, holding up his finished serape. "At least I've got something to show for my work. And soon I'll have a hat to go with it."

Nick approached his mom and waited for her to look up from her book. "How's the indexing going?" he asked.

"Good." She smiled. "You boys aren't still mad about being sent up to cut weeds, are you? That's important work too."

"It's okay. We actually got to help translate some Mayan writing." Carter and Angelo were watching him closely from the entrance, and he tried to wave them away. His mom was very good at realizing when he was up to something. "So, um, how often do they bring new stuff for you to look at?" he asked.

Mom took a bite of her meat. "I'm not sure. There hasn't been anything new since we started this morning. I think they're working on opening up some new rooms."

"Nothing?" Nick asked, his heart pounding. "Maybe they brought in some stuff last night before you started?"

"No. Everything has a tag with where it was found and when. It helps them keep track. One of the other catalogers was commenting on the fact that there hasn't been anything new for almost two days." She set her book down on the table and looked from Nick to his friends. A line formed above the bridge of her nose

127

that Nick recognized all too well. "Why are you asking these questions?"

"No reason." Nick kissed her on the cheek and backed quickly away. "Just wanted to make sure you're having a good time. Well, gotta go."

"Are you going to have dinner?" Dad asked, carrying an overloaded plate to the table.

"In just a minute," Nick said. "Dr. Canul asked us, to, uh, finish cutting a few more bushes."

Mom looked outside. "This late? It's nearly dark."

"That's why we have to hurry." Nick waved. "Gotta get it done while we can."

"That's the spirit," Dad said, digging into his meat. "Put in a good day's work and next thing you know, you'll be running the place."

"Do you think she believed you?" Angelo asked as Nick came out of the tent.

"Not a chance. She knows we're up to something. She just doesn't know what. But trust me, she'll be watching us close. So let's get out of here while we can." He started toward the pyramid of the sun.

"Hang on," Carter said, sniffing the cooking meat. "Aren't we going to have dinner?"

"No time," Nick said. "The best chance we have of getting away with this is sneaking in and out while everyone's eating."

Angelo pulled his monster notebook out of his pack. "Sneaking in and out of where?"

Nick broke into a jog. "Wherever they're hiding the stuff they took out of the pyramid."

"Where exactly are we going?" Carter asked, looking longingly over his shoulder at the camp that was quickly disappearing.

"No clue," Nick said.

To the west, the sun had finally set behind the forested hills and it was getting dark enough that it was hard to see where they were going. Angelo reached for his flashlight, but Nick held out a hand. "No lights."

Carter stopped so fast that Angelo bumped into him. "Hang on. Hang on. I don't like that we have to miss dinner. But I get that it's the best time to sneak out of camp without anyone noticing. I'm a little freaked out that you don't know where we're going. But hey, I'm not the one in charge of this adventure. But now you tell me we're heading randomly into the jungle with no one knowing where we are, *and* no light?"

Nick squatted on the ground and dug a couple of baseball-size rocks out of the soft dirt. He placed two of the rocks near each other. "Okay, let's say these are the pyramid of the sun and the pyramid of the moon."

"They don't look pointy enough to be pyramids,"

Carter said. "And the sides aren't nearly steep enough. Trust me, my legs still hurt."

Nick rolled his eyes. "Just imagine they're pointy and steep." He placed a third rock slightly away from the first two. "This is our camp. And this," he said, drawing a line in the grass, "is the road coming to our camp. Now, last night, what direction were the men carrying the boxes?"

Angelo thought for a minute. "Down the back side of the pyramid. Away from camp."

"Right." Nick tapped the far side of the two rocks. "Somewhere over here. They didn't bring the boxes back to camp or someone would have noticed. And they didn't take them away in any of the cars or someone would have heard it. If you're Dr. Canul and you want to hide alien artifacts, where would you keep them?"

Angelo tapped the ground on the opposite side of the pyramid of the sun. "Somewhere around here."

Nick nodded. "Which means a second camp. Which probably means more generators. All we have to do is hike around the pyramid and listen for the sound of generators."

"Why not just go over the top of the pyramid and down the other side?" Carter asked. "The same way the guys carrying the boxes went?"

Angelo took off his glasses, rubbing the lenses on his shirt. "We don't want the guards to see us."

"Guards?" Carter yelped. "You mean like big-muscled guys with guns and special forces training? No one said anything about guards."

Nick opened his mouth to say that the guards probably didn't have guns, and even if they did, they wouldn't shoot a bunch of defenseless kids. All the boys had to do was explain that they went for a walk before dinner and had gotten lost.

But he didn't need his speech. Carter jumped up and jogged toward the back of the pyramid, back bent and hands out to his sides. "Look out, forces of evil. You are no match for the cunning of Indiana Carter."

Nick looked at Angelo and the two of them grinned at each other in the dark. "Let's go kick some evil booty and recover the alien crystal skull," Nick said.

CHAPTER 14

TEN CUIDADO
DONDE PISAS

WATCH WHERE
YOU STEP

It turned out finding the hidden boxes wasn't quite as easy as listening for a generator. By the time the boys had gone around the pyramid and across the back twice, they were all exhausted.

"Let's take a break," Nick said, collapsing onto one of the pyramid's stone steps.

Angelo stared into the forest. "We'll never be able to hear the generators with all the noise coming from the animals out there."

Carter plopped down beside them. "I don't think I could hear anything over the growling of my stomach."

Angelo unzipped his pack and pulled out a bag of beef jerky. "Maybe this will help."

Carter's mouth dropped open like a ventriloquist puppet whose shoestring had just been pulled. "You've had beef jerky all this time and you didn't tell me? What kind of friend are you? That's like not telling a man dying of thirst in the middle of the desert that you have an ice-cold pitcher of cherry Kool-Aid."

Angelo dangled the bag in front of his friend's face. "Do you want it or not?"

Carter grabbed the bag, ripped it open, and shoved pieces of jerky into his mouth, making disgusting chewing noises.

Nick tilted his head to see if he could hear the voices he assumed must be ghostly spirits inside the pyramid. Fortunately, they seemed to be able to contact him only when he was inside too.

"Hearing the voices again?" Angelo asked.

Nick started. "I didn't tell you guys about the voices. How did you know?"

"It was either that or you were going crazy from jungle fever." Carter tilted his head. "Dude, you've been hearing dead people ever since you got turned into a zombie. It only makes sense you'd hear dead people around a pyramid, doesn't it?"

Nick gave an embarrassed smile. His friends knew him so well. "Yeah, but I've only heard them in graveyards. And even then, only when I could see the ghosts. I was thinking maybe I was . . ." He shrugged. "Imagining things. This place creeps me out."

Carter punched him lightly on the shoulder. "We believe you. Even if you are crazy."

"You heard them inside the pyramid of the moon today, didn't you?" Angelo asked. "That's how you knew what it said on the door."

Nick heaved a heavy sigh. "And last night in the pyramid of the sun. I was kind of hoping I'd imagined them. But then this morning . . ." He flapped his hands.

"Do you think they're . . . dead people? Inside the pyramids?" Carter asked around a mouthful of jerky.

Nick snorted. "If they're stuck inside there, I'm pretty sure they couldn't still be alive."

The boys sat and considered the idea of ghosts that were hundreds or thousands of years old speaking to Nick from inside an ancient Mayan pyramid. Nick had thought it was kind of cool talking to ghosts back in the graveyard near his home. But here in the middle of a jungle, far from anything familiar, it was so creepy it gave him chills.

"Could you understand them?" Angelo asked. "Or were they speaking Mayan?"

Nick scratched his cheek. "I don't think the dead

134

speak any specific language. I've been able to under-stand all the ghosts I've met."

"What did they say?"

Nick tried to remember. It was hard to pay attention when you were trying not to scream like a kindergart-ner. "Last night it was something about time. It's almost time or something like that."

Carter gulped down his jerky. "Time for what?"

"No clue. Today she said, 'Death is the start. And the time is close at hand.'"

"She?" Carter asked. "It was a girl?"

Nick bit the inside of his cheek. "I think so. It's kind of hard to tell. The voice was all whispery."

"'The time is close at hand,'" Angelo repeated. "The time for what?"

None of them had an answer. For all Nick knew, it could be time for the mummies to roll over in their cof-fins or rewrap their bandages or something.

"They could be people who were buried there," Angelo said. "Or maybe people who were sacrificed."

Nick shivered even though it wasn't all that cold.

"Or maybe," Carter said, "it's the ghosts of the first archaeologists. The ones who disappeared."

Nick stared at him. "*Seriously?*"

Carter coughed into his hand. "It was just a thought."

135

"Quiet, everybody." Angelo dropped to the ground.

For a moment Nick was sure Angelo had seen the very ghosts they'd been talking about. Then he spotted what Angelo had already seen. A line of men carrying more boxes down the back of the pyramid.

"It's them," Carter whispered.

"And they have more alien artifacts," Angelo said, his hands reaching down to touch the swabs tucked into the side of his pack.

Silently the boys watched the men hike down the side of the pyramid. When the men reached the bottom and walked into the jungle, Angelo jumped to his feet. "Come on," he whispered. "Let's follow them."

Heart racing, Nick followed Angelo through the tall grass and into the trees.

"You think we should split up?" Carter whispered. "Take them from three sides?"

"Are you crazy?" Nick gripped his arm. "We'd never find our way out."

As they stepped into the jungle, it was like someone had turned off a light. The moonlight and stars that had lit their way were blocked by the roof of leaves and branches above their heads. The boys froze and looked around. With dark shadows everywhere and a chorus of hoots, howls, and growls, surrounding them, it would

136

be all too easy to get completely disoriented.

Nick was about to suggest they leave and try again in the morning, when Carter pointed to the right. "Look! Isn't that lights?"

Nick squinted into the darkness, wondering if Carter had imagined it.

"There." Angelo pointed to a flickering light that appeared, moved down, and then disappeared.

"This way," he said, leading into the darkness.

Nick tried to follow, but he kept tripping over branches and catching his feet on roots. He tried not to think about the possibility that a jaguar might be tracking them or that a poisonous snake could be dangling just above their heads.

"Where did the lights go?" Carter said.

Nick had no idea. One minute they'd been bobbing around like fireflies, and the next minute they disappeared like birthday candles blown out on a kid's cake.

Cautiously the boys crept forward. "I can't see a thing," Nick whispered.

"Me either," Angelo said. "But they have to be around here somewhere."

Suddenly Carter stopped. "Do you smell that?"

Nick sniffed. He could smell something—sweet, and so strong it made his eyes water. It definitely wasn't a

137

flower. He took a step forward, and his foot came down on something that gave a hollow *clang* under his shoe.

All three boys froze in place.

"What was that?" Angelo said.

"I don't know," Nick whispered. He moved his foot back, knelt down, and was reaching to see what he had stepped on, when a metal door flew open, revealing a square of bright light. A man climbed out of the hole and called something in Spanish.

So close he could have reached out and touched the man's shoe, Nick froze. He didn't dare move an inch for fear the worker would look down and see him cowering on the ground. Without moving, he scanned his eyes left and right, looking for Carter and Angelo. But neither of them was anywhere in sight.

Another voice said something from inside the hole, and the first man looked down. As soon as he did, two sets of hands grabbed Nick and yanked him into the darkness. He nearly screamed before realizing it was Carter and Angelo. Silently, the three of them edged a safe distance into the trees.

"There's some kind of room down there," Carter whispered.

"No kidding," Nick said. "I was standing right on top of it when the door opened."

"It has to be where they keep the alien artifacts," Angelo said. "It looks like they're getting ready to leave. Once they do, we'll check it out."

One by one the workers emerged from the hole and headed back to the camp. Crouched in the bushes, the three boys waited. Nick kept glancing around behind him, sure a snake or a jaguar was about to attack.

When the generator shut off and the last man came out, Angelo stood up. "Let's go inside."

Cupping their flashlights to keep from being seen, the boys hurried back to the metal door. Nick was afraid it might be locked, but when Carter tugged on the plate it lifted silently.

"Keep an eye out for alarms or traps," Nick said.

"All over it," Carter said. "I'm like James Bond."

Nick rolled his eyes. "More like Mr. Bean."

Carter climbed down a ladder into the hole, and a moment later, his voice floated up. "Dude, this is awesome!"

Angelo hurried inside with Nick close behind. As soon as he stepped off the ladder and saw what was in the room, Nick gasped. The space was about the size of a railroad car. Shelves lined the walls from floor to ceiling, and every shelf was jammed full of vases, statues, cups, and jewelry of all shapes and sizes. There had to be millions of dollars' worth of treasure down there.

Carter grabbed a heavy gold necklace and started to jam it into his pocket.

"What are you doing?" Nick asked, stopping him.

"What? They stole it from the pyramid. Which means stealing it from them isn't a crime."

Nick held out his wrists as if they were handcuffed together. "Try telling that to the Mexican authorities when they discover you trying to sneak it past the airport customs."

Carter frowned, but he put the necklace back.

Angelo was in the corner examining a metal bowl. He touched something in the bowl and sniffed his fingers. "I don't think they're stealing things. It looks like they've been testing the treasures for something. The smell is from incense—a key piece of many Mayan religious rituals." He pointed his flashlight to a small book next to the bowl. "See how they're checking items in and out? It looks like they bring them here first, perform the ritual, then return them to camp."

"The item of power?" Nick said.

"That would be my guess." Angelo shined his light around the shelves. "I don't see any obvious alien artifacts. But some of this stuff clearly belonged to royalty. Look at this scepter, for example. If there *were* aliens,

140

their DNA has to be all over it." He gave Nick a handful of swabs and small plastic bags. "Help me get these things swabbed. Do the most royal-looking ones first. Like that crown over there. I'll test this scepter. Make sure and write down what you tested on each bag before you put the swabs in."

Carter picked up a long metal spear adorned with colorful feathers that were now mostly rotted away. "Me great hunter!"

"Don't touch that stuff," Angelo said. "We don't want to contaminate the DNA any more than it already has been."

By the time they were out of swabs, they had covered only a fraction of the items. "Should we go back and get more?" Nick asked.

Angelo tucked the baggies into his tester. "This is all I have. But there has to be some alien DNA on what we got."

"Check this out," Carter said, his voice echoing as if he had his head inside a metal pot. He stepped into the beam of Angelo's flashlight, his face hidden by a grotesque-looking demon mask. "How do I look?"

"Not much of a difference if you ask me," Nick said.

"Shh," Angelo hissed. He tilted his head, body tense. "Did you hear something?"

"You mean besides Carter?" Nick asked.

They waited for a moment before Angelo exhaled: "I thought I heard someone walking around out there. It was probably just the wind."

At that second there was an audible click and Nick froze. Slowly, the handle under the door turned. Before any of the boys could react, the metal plate swung open and a beam of light shined down inside.

142

CHAPTER 15

NO ME SIENTO
BIEN DE ESO

I HAVE A
BAD FEELING
ABOUT THIS

With nowhere to go, the boys froze as a pair of boots stepped through the door and onto the ladder. With his back to the boys, a man climbed into the hole. He was humming a happy tune, but Nick was sure that would stop when he turned around and saw he wasn't alone.

Nick looked for somewhere to go. But the ladder was the only way out, and there was no place to hide. He tried to think of some excuse for being there, but his brain was frozen. The only thing he was capable of thinking about was what the men would do once they discovered the boys knew their secret.

The man's left boot hit the concrete floor with a *thunk*. His right boot reached the floor and he let go of the ladder. As the worker began to turn, Carter grabbed the spear he'd been holding earlier. Still wearing the demon mask, he ran up to the man and let out a banshee wail that echoed off the walls of the enclosed space.

Thinking he was alone in the room, the man had to have thought he'd just come face-to-face with his most vivid nightmare. Behind a scruffy gray beard, his mouth dropped open. His eyes went wide, locked on the terrible face before him.

Carter shook the spear at the man and screamed again.

"*¡Diablo!*" the man howled. He grabbed the ladder and scrambled back out faster than Nick would have believed possible.

Carter yanked off the mask, dropped the spear, and started up the ladder behind him. "Run!" he screamed.

If the entire group had come back, there was no chance the boys would have managed to get away. But whether because he'd forgotten something and come back for it, or realized he had neglected to lock the door, the man appeared to be alone. He wouldn't be for long. By the time Nick, Carter, and Angelo got up the ladder, they could hear the worker screaming at the top of his lungs.

Running for their lives as they were, it was a miracle they managed to go in the right direction and none of them were separated. Sure the men would cut him and his friends off at any moment, Nick raced harder than he ever had in his life. It wasn't until they were back to the camp and hidden behind some tents that his legs gave out and he tumbled to the ground.

Carter and Angelo dropped beside him, all three of them gasping and panting. When his ears finally stopped ringing, Nick realized Carter was rolling back and forth on the ground. A thousand terrible possibilities filled his head. Had Carter been bit by something? Had he broken a bone? Had one of the men shot him?

Nick turned Carter over and realized his friend was laughing so hard that tears filled his eyes.

"That was amazing!" Carter said, clutching his stomach. "I've never been so scared in my life. Dude, that guy was so close I could smell his cologne. It was the worst stink ever. Like stench-of-the-jaguar's-bladder or something."

Suddenly Nick was laughing as well. "It probably wasn't cologne. I'll bet he peed his pants. I would have if you did that to me."

Angelo sat, clutching his ribs and gasping. "I thought

145

we were caught for sure. How did you come up with that?"

Carter wiped his eyes. "Desperation. The only thing I could think of was one time when I saw my sister tip-toeing down the hall at night to get a snack when we were both supposed to be in bed. I put on a werewolf mask and howled. It worked on her, so I figured it might work on him."

"Remind me never to sneak around your house at night," Nick said.

When they were finally breathing normally, the boys returned to their tent. Nick kept expecting some-one to drag them out, demanding to know what they'd been doing in the forest. But no one did, and the next morning everything seemed like business as usual.

Mr. Jiménez met them for breakfast and informed them with a smile and a shrug that they'd be back cut-ting weeds on the pyramid of the moon. "Work hard and maybe Dr. Canul will give you a break."

"I don't get it," Nick said under his breath. "Why isn't anybody saying anything about what we saw last night?"

"They might not know it was us," Carter suggested. "You were in the dark when the guy opened the door, and we ran like crazy."

Angelo cut into a thick Mexican sausage the cook had called *chorizo*. "Or perhaps they know it was us, but admitting we were there would mean admitting they've been trying to find the alien artifact."

Nick wondered if Dr. Lopez would meet them at the temple again. But apparently she was working somewhere else. He didn't blame her. If anything, it was hotter than the day before, and the bugs were even more annoying.

As soon as they reached the top of the pyramid, Carter took out his knitting, and Angelo began passing around the temple. He'd seemed tense all morning, and Nick was pretty sure he knew why. "I'm sure your test will come back for alien DNA this time. But if even they, you know, don't . . . that doesn't mean you have to stop hunting monsters. It just means we need to find proof of some other monster to show your parents."

"Sure," Angelo said. But he continued to pace. Nick had to find a way to take his friend's mind off the swabs before he burst a brain cell or something.

"Tell me more about that book," he said, snipping a few random leaves. "The purple view of something."

"*Popol Vuh*," Angelo said absently. "Why do you want to know? I thought you didn't care about it."

Nick didn't. But he knew if he could get Angelo

147

talking about something, it would calm him down. "Well, if there is a secret passage to the alien artifact like you said, maybe this book has a clue about how to find it. Or . . ." He had an idea he knew Angelo would like. "What if the item isn't a device to summon the spaceship? What if it's an actual portal to their planet?"

Angelo stopped pacing. "That could be. The passageway is an actual passageway. An alien species advanced enough to fly to Earth might very well have the ability to create a doorway home once they got here."

He grabbed his monster notebook and began flipping through its pages. "From what I've read, the *Popol Vuh* mostly seems to be a story about these two brothers who go to the underworld and have to pass all these tests. Their uncles tried before them, only they failed when they were sent into something called the house of darkness and burned torches they were commanded not to."

Carter came over to listen. "Got any more of that jerky?"

"What happens to them after they fail?" Nick asked.

Angelo pulled the half-empty bag out of his pack. "The lords of death cut off one of their heads and hang it in a tree. But the hero brothers pass all the tests and get past the lords of death."

They shared the jerky and sat in the shade as Angelo told the tale of how the hero brothers passed the tests. It was pretty cool. There was a head hanging from a tree that spit into a woman's hand, ten scary demons, and a bunch of exciting obstacles.

By the time Angelo got to the end, Nick was leaning back against the wall, feeling a little sleepy.

Carter fished through the bag for any last jerky crumbs.

"Did you know the last party of archaeologists came here at almost the exact same time of year as this group?" Angelo said, stifling a yawn.

"Weird coincidence," Nick said, tugging halfheartedly at a root between his feet.

"Actually, it might not be," Angelo said. "I mean, what are the odds that both teams arrived within a few days of the same date?"

Carter sucked jerky dust from his fingers. "They probably both had time off for Christmas break."

Angelo shook his head. "I don't think it had anything to do with Christmas. I think Dr. Lopez was right—it's all about the winter solstice. It's like everything here was built to be a huge calendar." He pulled out the black folder and studied one of the newspaper clippings. "Okay, this is really strange. The team of archaeologists who were lost almost definitely disappeared during the exact day of the winter solstice fifty-two years ago. And tonight is the winter solstice too. Coincidence?"

The root Nick was pulling on suddenly came loose, and he fell against the wall. He rubbed his spine and lay back on the grass. "What are you saying? You think something's going to happen here again?"

"I don't know," Angelo said, returning to the pages. "But I think it might be interesting to find our way to the top of the pyramid of the sun tonight. Maybe just hang around and see what happens."

"Sure. Why not?" Nick closed his eyes and yawned. "What's the worst that could happen?"

The next thing he knew, someone was shaking him.

"Wake up," Angelo said. "We fell asleep."

Nick sat up and realized the sun was almost all the way across the sky. "What time is it?"

Angelo checked his tablet. "After five. Come on. We need to check the DNA tester."

"Not until we eat." Carter groaned and rubbed his stomach. "I'm starving."

It was all they could do to keep Angelo from going

straight back to the tent. When they dragged him to dinner, he hunched over his reading and barely touched his food. Carter finished off the last of his tacos and eyed Angelo's plate. "Are you going to eat those?"

Angelo pushed his plate to Carter. "This is amazing."

"I know, right?" Carter said. "I don't think I'll ever be able to eat at Taco Bell after this. The cook is, like, some kind of magician."

"Not the food," Angelo said. "These pages. There's a whole article on ceremonies. According to this, some people believed you could draw power directly from a god if you were his direct descendant. A few of the royalty even believed they could *become* the god by taking the life of an innocent person. What if the aliens had a way of turning the Mayan leaders into their species? Or what if the kings really were aliens, but no one knew it because they disguised themselves as humans?"

Nick was only half listening. There was something odd going on in the meal tent, but he couldn't put his finger on what it was. "Do you guys notice anything different around here?" he asked.

Carter and Angelo looked around. "What do you mean, *different*?" Carter said. "Like, *Hey we're all wearing matching shirts* different or *Look, that guy has two heads* different?"

151

"I'm not sure." Nick looked at the men talking and eating at a nearby table. There was a sort of nervous intensity to their words and actions—as if they were all waiting for something.

"You know how a group of people will line up at a theme park when a new ride opens? Everyone's kind of talking excitedly and watching the gate. Then, as soon as they start letting people in, the energy rises to this whole new level. That's what this feels like."

"They're probably waiting for more tacos," Carter said. "I know I am."

Angelo studied the men around them. "I see what you mean. It's like a bunch of wasps after someone has poked their nest. You think it has something to do with what we saw last night?"

Nick wasn't sure. But whatever it was, it made him uncomfortable.

"Let's get back to the tent and do those tests," Nick said. "Then I want to find my mom and dad. I don't know what's going on here. But I don't like it."

Back at their tent, Angelo quickly inserted the tubes into the tester and started up the machine. Nick dropped onto his cot and something crackled. "What's this?" he asked, pulling a piece of white paper out from under his leg.

It was a note. Nick read it with a sense of unease.

152

Having dinner with Dr. Canul on top of the
pyramid of the sun. Don't get into any trouble.

The note must have been written by his dad—the letters weren't neat enough to be his mom's.

"Everything okay?" Carter asked.

Nick nodded. "I guess. It's just . . ."

The tester started beeping and Angelo pulled out the results. He scanned them quickly and frowned. "Guys, I think we have a problem."

CHAPTER 16

NO ME SIENTO BIEN DE ESO TAMPOCO

I HAVE A BAD FEELING ABOUT THAT TOO

"What's up?" Carter asked. "Did you discover alien DNA?"

"No," Angelo said. "No alien DNA at all. It looks like I've been wrong about the extraterrestrials all along."

"You don't know that," Nick said. "Maybe there is alien DNA and you just haven't found any yet."

Angelo sighed. "It doesn't matter. I'm out of swabs. There's no way I can prove extraterrestrials were ever here."

Carter grabbed his shoulder. "I'm sorry, man."

Angelo looked up from the tester, his eyes wide. He licked his lips. "But I did find something else. Remember how I told you guys that Mayan royalty believed they were descended directly from the gods?"

Nick nodded, wondering why Angelo was going off on a tangent again.

Angelo held up the paper, covered with numbers that meant nothing to Nick. "When I took the swabs, I was searching for nonhuman DNA. I didn't find that. But the test results show something strange." He pointed at one set of numbers. "This is the DNA I took off my hard hat. And this is the set of DNA I took from the scepter I found in the underground room. Look at these two. They're not identical, but they're a close enough match that it can't be a coincidence."

Carter waved his hands in a hurry-up gesture. "You're doing that *I'm a really smart scientist, so no one can understand me* thing again. Talk in sixth-grade words."

Angelo set down the paper. "These tests suggest that someone who touched my hard hat is a direct descendant of someone who was in the pyramid hundreds of years ago."

"Canul," Nick said. "He bragged about being a direct descendant of the Mayans and he gave us the hats."

"That's what I think too," Angelo said. "Only, what if he's not just a descendant of the people who built the pyramid, but the king himself? It would explain how protective he is of everything here. And if that's the case, he might believe the myths about being a direct descendant of the sun god, too."

The pieces that had been swirling in Nick's head snapped together with a bang. "The incense in the underground room, the winter solstice, the voices saying it was almost time. He's going to try to perform a ceremony to get the power of the sun god."

"Not just the sun god's power," Angelo said. "I think he's trying to *become* the sun god. What if that's what his father was trying to do fifty-two years ago, too?"

"That could be why everybody disappeared," Carter said. "Maybe something went wrong."

Nick's mouth went dry, and his tongue stuck to the roof of his mouth. "My parents are with Dr. Canul right now, on top of the pyramid. What if that's why he brought us here? He could be getting ready to use my parents as some kind of sacrifice!"

For a second Nick could only stand there. His parents . . . on a pyramid . . . about to be sacrificed to the sun god. It was like something straight out of all the horror movies he'd ever seen.

"We have to call the police!" Carter shouted, pacing frantically around the tent.

Angelo clutched the DNA results in one fist. "What police? And how would we call them?"

Nick walked to the entrance of the tent. "We have to tell *someone*."

"But who do we tell?" Angelo stood up. "Canul is in charge of the excavation. For all we know, the whole camp is in on it."

"Then we handle it ourselves." Nick ran out of the tent and straight into Mr. Jiménez.

"Whoa," the little man said, catching Nick. "What's the hurry?"

Angelo and Carter came running out behind Nick, and Mr. Jiménez seemed to realize something was really wrong. "What's going on here? Did something happen?"

Nick wasn't sure who he could trust, but they needed help and they couldn't stand around while his parents were in danger. "It's my mom and dad," Nick gasped. "Dr. Canul has them on top of the pyramid and he's going to sacrifice them."

The archaeologist started to smile. "This is a joke of some kind? Yes?"

"It's not a joke," Carter said. "He's trying to do some crazy hocus-pocus stuff to get the power of the sun god."

Mr. Jiménez looked from Nick to Carter, the smile disappearing from his face.

"It's true," Angelo said. "I took a swab from an

157

ancient scepter. The DNA is a direct match to someone in the camp. It has to be Dr. Canul."

"Let me see that," Mr. Jiménez said, reaching for the DNA results. Angelo handed him the strip of paper, and the archaeologist studied it carefully. He rubbed the top of his bald head. "This does appear valid. But it's quite a leap to go from a DNA test to human sacrifice. Dr. Canul is a respected archaeologist."

"It's not just the DNA," Angelo said. He took the black folder from his backpack. "It's all in here. The first group of archaeologists disappeared during the winter solstice. They were doing the same thing. But something must have happened."

Mr. Jiménez took the folder and glanced through the pages. "Where did you get this?"

"Does it matter?" Nick asked, bouncing from one foot to the other. "If you're not coming with us, we're going on our own. My parents could be in danger."

"Yes, all right." The archaeologist took a handkerchief from his pocket and wiped the perspiration from his face. "I still don't believe Dr. Canul is capable of something like this. But we'd better check it out just the same." He turned and hurried toward the pyramid.

"Shouldn't we get some help?" Angelo asked.

"If what you say is true, we may not have time. The kind of ceremony you are talking about would require preparation. Besides . . ." He glanced over his shoulder at Nick and his friends as they climbed the pyramid. "I hate to admit it, but I've had a suspicion something was going on for a while now. I have no idea who else might be involved."

The four of them hurried up the steps of the pyramid as the sun turned first red and then orange, dipping low in the sky.

"Tell him about the underground room," Carter panted.

Nick checked with Angelo, still not sure how much they should be sharing. When Angelo nodded, Nick told Mr. Jiménez about seeing the men taking boxes from the pyramid and following them to the underground room in the jungle. The more he told, the angrier the archaeologist grew.

"This is unacceptable! These are priceless artifacts." He threw out his arms. "They should be in a museum, not in a . . . a *bunker*!"

"A *stinky* bunker," Carter said.

"Eh?" Mr. Jiménez raised an eyebrow.

"It smelled like they were burning incense," Angelo said.

The archaeologist jerked as if he'd been slapped. "No."

"Does that mean something?" Nick asked. His chest

159

felt like it was on fire and he had a cramp in his side, but he had to keep pushing.

"It *could*," Mr. Jiménez said, without explaining any further.

As soon as they reached the top of the pyramid, Nick looked toward the altar where he and his family had eaten dinner with Dr. Canul. There was no sign of the doctor or his parents. "Where are they?" he asked, unsure whether to be relieved or worried even more.

Mr. Jiménez pointed to Nick and Carter. "You two check the sides and back of the temple." He nodded toward Angelo. "You and I will look inside. Perhaps this is simply a miscommunication."

As Mr. Jiménez and Angelo started into the temple, the archaeologist looked back. "If you see anything, call out. Do *not* try to handle it on your own."

Nick chewed on his bottom lip. Something was wrong. Even if his parents had joined Dr. Canul for an innocent dinner, why weren't they here? "You go left and I'll go right," he said. "If you see them shout for me."

Carter bunched his fists. "If I see that gasbag messing with your mom, I'll hit him so hard his grandkids will feel it."

Nick jogged the grassy stone surface of the pyramid.

160

The sun was almost down now and he was growing more and more worried by the second. As he rounded the back of the temple, he thought he heard something. "Carter?" he called.

Carter raced around from the other side of the building, his face red with exertion. "Did you see something?"

"No. You?"

Carter shook his head and ran his hands through his red, green, and white–striped hair. "Maybe they ate already and went back to camp?"

"Could be." Nick glanced toward the back of the temple. Mr. Jiménez and Angelo should have been able to search it by now. "Let's see if they found anything."

When the two boys reached the back entrance of the temple, the sun was nothing more than a gold splinter in a deep purple sky. They stopped just outside the arched doorway. "Angelo?" Nick called. "Mr. Jiménez?"

There was no answer.

"I don't like this," Carter said.

Nick didn't either. "Careful," he whispered, stepping into the dark building.

"Right behind you," Carter said.

Squinting to try to make out anyone who might be lurking in the shadows, Nick walked as quietly as he

161

could from room to room. Twice he thought he heard something—a shuffling of feet or heavy breathing. Both times, when he stopped, the noise disappeared.

"Why are you stopping?" Carter asked the second time.

"I don't know. I thought I heard something."

"Let's go outside," Carter said, his voice high and tense. "I keep feeling like someone's sneaking up on me."

Nick felt the exact same way. It was too dark. Too closed in. Even with most of the plants cleared away, it felt like there were hiding places everywhere. Besides, by now Angelo and Mr. Jiménez were no doubt looking for them outside.

Trying to breathe silently, Nick hurried through the rest of the temple rooms. When he got to the main entrance, he gave a sigh of relief. "I guess they're not up here." He turned back to Carter, but there was no one behind him.

"Carter?" he called, stepping back into the entrance. There was no answer. "Carter!" he shouted.

Something scraped across the stone floor behind him, and he turned just as an arm looped around his neck. Nick struggled to get away, but the arm pulled him up and backward until his toes barely touched

162

the ground. Something sharp poked his left shoulder. He opened his mouth to scream but couldn't inhale enough air. His head began to swim and all at once his legs would no longer hold him up.

"Run!" he tried to shout, but the words never made it past his lips. His eyelids began to droop closed. A figure stepped in front of him. He recognized the face grinning down at him. It was Mr. Jiménez.

163

CHAPTER 17

SIEMPRE DEBES
CONFIAR EN TUS
SENTIMIENTOS

**ALWAYS TRUST
YOUR FEELINGS**

Nick woke with a pounding headache. He tried to roll over but couldn't move. Slowly he managed to crack open his eyelids. It took him a minute or two to focus. When he did, he discovered that he was lying on his back facing the starry night sky. He began to sit up before realizing his arms and legs were tied with thick yellow rope.

"Where am I?" he tried to ask. But a cloth was jammed between his teeth. With a start, he remembered everything. The pyramid, his parents, Carter and Angelo. Yanking at the ropes, he began to cough. The coughing turned into choking and he couldn't breathe.

A hand removed the gag from his mouth, and he

gasped for air. Mr. Jiménez stared down at him.

"Help!" he screamed. Jiménez slapped a hand over his mouth.

"I can leave the gag in place," the man said. "Maybe you choke. Maybe you don't. It matters little to me." He peered cheerfully down at Nick as though the two of them were discussing whether to have hot dogs or hamburgers for dinner. "Or I can take the gag off and you agree to no more shouting. What do you say?"

Nick wanted to tell the archaeologist to eat rocks, but he knew the chance of suffocating with the gag in his mouth was real. "Okay," he said. With the man's palm pressed against his mouth, it came out as *rrmm-kaw*, so he nodded vigorously to make sure Jiménez understood him.

Slowly Jiménez removed his hand. Nick gulped in the night air. "Much better," the man said. He looked left. "That wasn't so hard, was it?"

Nick turned his head to see Angelo and Carter bound and gagged on the ground a few feet away. At the same time, he realized he was several feet above the ground. *Oh, no.* He was tied to the top of the stone altar outside the temple of the sun.

"What about you two?" Jiménez said to Carter and Angelo. "Can you follow this fine boy's example?"

Both of them nodded, and the archaeologist removed their gags as well. "Don't make me put these back in or I might forget to leave you room to breathe."

"It was *you*," Carter spat as soon as his mouth was free. "You're the one who set this all up."

Jiménez chuckled. "It's funny. People see a tall man, piercing eyes, the doctor before his name, and they naturally assume Dr. Canul is the one in charge of things here. Let that be a lesson to you boys—never judge a man by his title."

"What did you do to my parents?" Nick asked.

"Why, nothing." Jiménez walked around the altar and rested against its base so he could watch all three of them at the same time. "Right about now they're on top of the pyramid with Dr. Canul, finishing an exceptional dinner."

Nick craned his neck to look around, but the archaeologist held up a dusty finger. "Not on *this* pyramid. That would never do. I'm afraid I told a teensy lie when I left the note in your tent. You see, I suggested that Dr. Canul take your parents to dinner on top of the pyramid of the moon, now that you've gone to so much trouble cleaning it off. I made sure to explain that when the moon hit just the right point it would shine through the temple and into the mirrors below the entrance."

Nick tried to roll over, but he was tied so well he could barely squirm. "Why?"

Mr. Jiménez smiled pleasantly, but Nick thought it was the smile of a serial killer. "I'm glad you asked." He checked his watch and glanced up at the sky. "We've got a few minutes."

"Until you kill us?" Nick growled.

The archaeologist gasped, appearing shocked, although Nick was sure it was nothing but an act. "I promise not to lay a hand on your heads." He opened his bag and took out Angelo's monster notebook with the black folder inside.

"Be careful with that," Angelo said. "I've been working on it for years."

Jiménez took out the folder and dropped the notebook on the ground. "I don't think you'll be needing it." He flipped through the pages in the folder. "This is actually much more information than I would have preferred you have. It could have made things . . . *uncomfortable* if you'd put the pieces together much earlier. But now that we're all together, it makes the explanation quite a bit quicker."

He flipped through the pages. "Where did you say you got this?"

"We don't know," Angelo said. "Someone left it for

167

us at the hotel. I sort of thought it might have been you."

Jiménez gave him a narrowed-eyed glare. "It doesn't matter." He let the folder fall, and several of the pages fluttered off in the breeze—a breeze that was picking up with each passing moment.

"Aren't you afraid someone will find that?" Nick asked.

"Not at all." The archaeologist laughed. He checked his watch again. "Very soon, it won't matter who knows what."

Angelo twisted around and managed to sit up. "You're delusional if you think you can get the power of the sun god."

"Not delusional at all. As I told you, I'm from a small village less than twenty miles away. Even though this site was officially closed, I came here often. I wondered what had happened to the first group of explorers who disappeared so mysteriously. But it wasn't until I was ready to leave for college that my father told me the truth."

Nick tested the ropes binding his hands, but they were tied solidly. "How would your father know what happened?"

"Didn't I tell you? The two people who left the first expedition before that fateful night fifty-two years ago? One of them was my grandfather. He'd been added to

168

the party late as a simple laborer. No one had a clue that he knew more about Mayan history than all the rest of those so-called experts combined. The other man was my father. He was just a boy at the time. They didn't know nearly as much as I do. But they knew enough to understand a calamity was about to happen."

"They knew the archaeologists were going to try to open the portal," Angelo said.

"They didn't try." Jiménez grinned a sly and know-ing smile. "They succeeded. Dr. Canul's father, Samuel Canul, was considered a bit of a nutcase by both his colleagues and his family. He had some strange ideas about demons, dark magic, that sort of thing. He had just enough real knowledge to come here, where he found this book." He held up a thick book made of metal plates.

"Is that the purple view?" Nick asked.

Jiménez laughed out loud. "The *Popol Vuh*? Nothing so simple as that."

"It's instructions on how to open the portal to the underworld," Angelo said. "You plan to open the door-way at the exact moment of the winter solstice and get past the demons to become a god. Let me guess, you found the king's item of power to let you defeat the demons."

Mr. Jiménez clapped his hands slowly. "Very good. I could see a very successful career in your future. *If* you had a future."

"What do you mean?" Carter asked. "You said you wouldn't hurt us."

"Oh, *I* won't." The archaeologist pretended to wipe a tear from his eye. "Unfortunately bad things tend to befall those who are still around when the portal to Xibalba is opened. That's what happened to Samuel Canul and everyone in his party. They knew enough to open the portal, but Canul didn't understand he had zero chance of obtaining the power of the gods. Now they're somewhere in the depths below us. The same place where Dr. Canul and all his loyal archaeologists will end up."

"What if the item of power doesn't work?" Carter asked desperately.

Jiménez steepled his fingers in front of his chest and nodded. "Oh, it will work. You see, to become a god, you need more than just the item. You must be a direct descendant of royalty. Despite his claims to the contrary, Samuel Canul was as much a descendant of the king as I am of Santa Claus."

Angelo shook his head. "But my test said . . ." He sucked in his breath. "It was *your* DNA I found. Not Dr.

Canul's. You touched the hard hats when you got them for him out of the supply tent."

Jiménez laughed again. It was like listening to a poisonous snake rattling before it attacked. "I knew you boys were smart. Poor Dr. Canul may well be of Mayan descent. But he is certainly no royalty. I, on the other hand, can trace my lineage directly back to—"

"The king?" Carter said.

"No." Jiménez dropped his head. "Sadly, the king never had any children. He died as a child. And with his mother and father both dead—some say at the hands of assassins, others suspect someone a little closer—the line of royalty went to the only living relative, the child's uncle, his father's brother. And as it turns out, I am a direct descendant of his."

"But—" Angelo started, then snapped his jaws shut.

A flash of light lit the sky not far away and Jiménez looked sharply up. "Time is short and I'm afraid my story must be too. Suffice it to say, my grandfather discovered what Canul planned to do. He also knew the good doctor was not a descendant of royalty. He and my father escaped, then came back to gather all the party's papers, and this book I now hold." Overhead, the sky was growing dark as wind began to blow in earnest.

"The newspapers said there was no evidence of the camp found," Angelo said.

"There wasn't once my father and grandfather took what they wanted and destroyed the rest to keep anyone from coming back and doing the same thing. Of course, once my father told me what had happened—along with our lineage—I was obsessed with the subject. I'm the one who figured out that the opportunity to become a god didn't happen every winter solstice at all. Only every fifty-two years—a cycle the Mayans called *xiuhmolpilli*. I'm the one who realized that if I was here—and prepared—I could use that portal to become a god. From that point on, it was only a matter of pulling the right strings, paying a few bribes, letting Dr. Canul think the expedition was his idea, and here we are."

He looked up to where dark clouds now covered the sky in a menacing black blanket. A drop of rain hit Nick on the nose, but he couldn't reach up to wipe it away. "Fine. You're an egotistical psycho who thinks he can become a god. But why bring a family all the way here from California?"

"That was the tricky part." The archaeologist held up his hand, like a professor teaching a class. "You see, at first I thought opening the entryway to the

172

underworld required a simple sacrifice. I'd have felt bad killing someone to get what I wanted. But . . ." He flapped his hands. "I'd get over it. Then I did more research—in the kinds of books archaeology professors don't teach from. That's when I discovered there was one more piece to the ceremony. The life of someone with no Mayan blood was the price that had to be paid."

Lightning struck again. At least Nick thought it was lightning. But he'd never seen green lightning bolts before. "Sorry," Jiménez said. "Story time is over. Let the show begin." He reached into a leather bag on the ground and pulled out a long, sharp knife.

Nick tried to pull away as the archaeologist approached the altar. "You promised you weren't going to touch me."

"I'm not." Jiménez raised the knife and cut the palm of his hand. As soon as blood began to flow from the shallow wound, he pressed his hand to the top of the stone altar. "The blood of royalty," he whispered in a flat, almost mechanical, voice.

He reached into the bag again, took out four stone vases, and set them on the ground on each side of the altar. Around the pyramid, the wind began to blow even harder as the man placed sticks of incense into

173

each vase and lit them. "North, south, east, and west," he said in the same voice. Lightning split the sky again, and the animal sounds from the rain forest rose to an earsplitting pitch.

Nick tried to pull free of his ropes, but the knots were too tight. "If you don't want my blood, what do you want?" he hollered over the sound of the wind and the jungle.

"It's not your blood I need," Jiménez yelled back, clasping the book to his chest. "It's your life energy. Your drive, your will to live, your brains."

Although the tropical wind was still hot, the rain was cold and quickly turned to hail. Bits of ice pounded Nick's face, and he turned his head. Carter and Angelo were staring at him with open terror.

Angelo struggled in his ropes. "Take me!" he screamed. "Take my life force, not Nick's. I'm the one who got us into this."

"What are you talking about?" Nick yelled.

"If I hadn't been so focused on aliens for my own selfish reasons, we would have figured this out long before now. I was busy reading books about heroes and demons when the truth was right in front of me." He turned to Jiménez. "You said you needed brains. No offense, but I'm the smartest kid I know."

Jiménez looked from Angelo to the sky. "You make a good point. We might just have time."

"No!" Nick screamed. But with his hands and feet tied, there was nothing he could do to stop Jiménez as the archaeologist shoved him off the altar and dragged an unresisting Angelo onto it.

Holding the metal book open in front of him, the archaeologist began chanting words Nick couldn't understand. He assumed it was Mayan or something even older. As the archaeologist finished reading the last of the words, he held the book above his head, shouted something, and looked to the sky. The wind blew so hard it took Nick's breath away. Hail covered the ground. And then . . . everything stopped.

All at once the wind quit blowing, the rain ceased, and the sky cleared.

Nick looked at Jiménez, waiting for some kind of miraculous change. The archaeologist stood, chest out, hands holding the book above his head, face toward the sky.

The rain forest returned to its normal cheeps, chatters, and howls.

"Well," Carter said, leaning forward. "Are you a god?"

Slowly Jiménez lowered the book. He looked at

himself, then down at the altar. Watching his face crumple was like watching a kid learning he wasn't getting any presents for his birthday. He seemed so lost, Nick almost felt sorry for him.

The archaeologist stumbled backward, fell against the altar, and muttered, "It didn't work."

CHAPTER 18

MI MADRE NUNCA HIZO ESTO

MY MOTHER NEVER DID THIS

Mr. Jiménez studied the book before letting it slowly fall to the ground. He stared at his hands as if he'd never seen them before. "I don't understand. I did everything right. It should have worked. I did the research."

Carter wormed himself into a sitting position. "So, um, did you ever consider the possibility that you're, you know, *completely crazy*, and people don't actually get superpowers unless they're bitten by radioactive spiders?"

"What?" Jiménez looked around, seeming to realize for the first time that Nick and his friends were still there. He grabbed the book and knife, and Nick was afraid the archaeologist was going to kill them after all.

Instead, he shoved the items quickly into his bag and looked around as though wondering who else might have seen him. "Now listen," he said with a nervous laugh. "I know what you all must be thinking."

"That you're a complete psychopath?" Carter suggested.

"You've got the wrong idea." Jiménez shot a considering glance at each of the boys, and appeared to make up his mind. He hurried around the altar, picking up the incense holders. "Weren't you boys telling me just this morning how bored you were? How you wanted some adventure?"

Nick didn't recall anything like that, but he wanted to see what the man had in mind—especially if it didn't involve killing him and his friends. He nodded as best he could while still being tied up. "Sure. I remember that."

The archaeologist licked his lips. "You wanted excitement. I provided it. I was thinking just this afternoon that we hadn't really shown you a good time. Dr. Canul is such a stick-in-the-mud. But this is your vacation. So, I thought, hey, why not give you something to remember? A little playacting."

"You're saying you drugged and kidnapped us because we were *bored*?" Angelo asked, clearly not believing a word of it.

Mr. Jiménez forced out a laugh. "A mild sedative. To make the whole thing more believable. Did it work? Did you believe I was actually trying to trade your life force for the power of the sun god?"

"I tell you what I believe," Carter said. "I believe you're a total—"

"Totally great actor," Nick interrupted. "That was amazing, with the chanting and the incense. I absolutely thought it was real." He gave his friends a meaningful look. "Didn't you guys?"

Angelo was the first to catch on. He winked at Nick. "I might have believed it for the first few minutes. When I woke up gagged and tied up, I thought it was real. But then when you started making up all that obvious fake Mayan stuff, I realized it was only an act. It was exciting though."

"*Fake?*" Mr. Jiménez huffed indignantly, then chuckled. "I mean, well, I had to make it seem real, didn't I?"

Carter's forehead crinkled. He frowned at Nick and Angelo, before understanding crossed his face. "Yeah, it was totally cool. I especially liked the cutting-your-hand thing. Only, how did you make it storm like that?"

The archaeologist's smile froze. "I, um, well . . . It's a rain forest. Storms happen all the time."

"It was great!" Nick said, hoping his enthusiasm didn't sound as forced as it felt. He held out his tied

179

arms. "Now that it's over, you better untie us. My parents are probably getting worried." Once they were free, the first thing he would do was tell anyone who'd listen what a raving maniac Mr. Jiménez really was.

Perhaps the archaeologist heard something in Nick's voice. Or maybe he wasn't quite as gullible as he seemed. His eyes narrowed and he rubbed his chin thoughtfully. "You know, if I were to release the three of you, and you tried to claim this was anything more than a fun little game, it could get *awkward* for all of us."

"What kind of awkward?" Angelo asked.

Mr. Jiménez reached into his bag and removed the metal book. "The kind where the wrong conclusions might be made. I have strong connections with the state authorities. It would be quite unfortunate for you—and your parents—if the *policía federal* were to get the impression that outsiders had attempted to steal national treasures."

Nick's gut went cold. "If we say anything about what happened here, you tell the police we tried to steal that book?"

"Among other things. Your mother and father have spent the last two days with their hands on all manner of valuable items. It would be a shame if some of them turned up in your tent."

"That's blackmail!" Carter shouted, yanking at his

ropes. "Nick's mom and dad would never steal any-thing. And neither would we."

"Take it or leave it," Jiménez warned. He put the book back into his bag and took out the knife. He turned it left and right, the blade flashing silver in the light of the moon. "Do you agree to say nothing about what happened here? Or do I find another way to shut the three of you up?"

They didn't seem to have much of a choice. "Fine," Nick said. "Get these ropes off us."

Jiménez grinned and cut the three boys free. "Don't forget," he snarled. "One wrong word and you and your family spend the next twenty years in a Mexican prison."

Nick turned and stomped away with Carter. Angelo stopped to grab his monster notebook. "Where's my backpack?"

"And my hat?" Carter demanded. "I'm not leaving my yarn and needles behind."

"It's all in the temple," Jiménez said, looking more than a little flustered. "We can come back for it in the morning."

"If we all rush him, we can take him down," Carter whispered. "Then we can tie him up and tell everyone what really happened."

Nick shook his head. "He's probably got a dozen

181

men ready to swear he was with them all night. Right now, Jiménez has the power. But once we get back home, I'm going to do everything I can to make sure he gets punished."

"I knew that guy didn't have any idea what he was doing," Carter said. "He probably copied that ceremony from some old horror movie."

"It was real," Angelo said.

Nick and Carter stared at him like he'd gone as crazy as Jiménez.

Angelo leaned close and whispered, "The reason it didn't work wasn't because it was fake. It's because his blood isn't royal." He flipped open his monster notebook and turned to a page where he'd been copying pictures from the different carvings they'd seen. He pointed to a drawing of a line of people, one above the other. "Remember this?"

"Yeah," Carter said. "It was on the wall of the temple of the moon. What did you call it? A Jenny something?"

"Genealogy," Angelo said, making sure to speak softly enough that Jiménez couldn't overhear him. "It's a lineage of power passed from one king to another. See, here on the bottom is the child king buried in the pyramid. Above that is his father, grandfather, and so on. Look at the second-to-last picture—the baby's father

182

who was killed along with his wife. I didn't notice at the time, but see to the left where his siblings should be? According to this, he had only a sister, not a brother. When the king and his wife were killed, his sister would have been charged with looking after the baby."

"So it wasn't the king's uncle who had the power," Nick said. "It was his aunt. Which means her husband was royalty by marriage, not by birth. The mummy's uncle didn't have royal blood, and Jiménez doesn't either." He thought for a minute. "How could Jiménez not have realized that?"

"Everyone's been so focused on the pyramid of the sun, they never took time to study the pyramid of the moon. And you know what? I think the royal family might have been buried there. Why else would the entrance be sealed off?"

Carter brushed a few stray pieces of hail out of his hair. "But if Jiménez didn't have royal blood, why didn't we all disappear like the first group of explorers did?"

Angelo glanced up toward the pyramid of the moon. "Maybe we still will."

By the time they reached the base of the pyramid, they could tell something was wrong. Lights were on all over the camp, and a small crowd was gathered outside the meal tent.

"They're probably organizing a search party to come find us," Angelo said.

But as one of the men moved aside, Nick spotted a familiar figure sprawled out on a cot. "Mom!" he screamed, racing through the crowd. His mom was lying down in front of the tent with thick white bandages wrapped around the top of her head.

He skidded to a stop at her side, and she looked up at him and smiled weakly. "There you are. I was worried about you."

"Worried about *me*?" He reached out to her bandaged forehead, then pulled back his fingers, afraid he would hurt her. "What happened? What did Dr. Canul do to you?"

Carter turned to face the crowd, arms raised in a boxing stance. "Where is he? I'll make him wish he'd never been born."

Dr. Canul stepped out of the tent. "Your mother slipped and hit her head. It's possible she has a slight concussion, but she's going to be fine."

Nick's mom nodded. "It's true. We were finishing our dinner when it started to rain. Dr. Canul suggested we go into the temple. We went inside and there was a bright flash—lightning, I guess. I tripped and hit my head on the altar. But I'm fine, really. I just feel a little . . . woozy."

Carter lowered his fists, and Nick's shoulders slumped with relief. "Where's Dad?" he asked.

"Over here." Nick turned to see his dad sitting in a nearby camp chair. He was bent over, head in his hands.

"Are you okay?" Nick asked.

Dad moaned and rubbed the back of his neck. "On top of the pyramid, I started feeling sick. My head is spinning and my stomach feels like I ate six corn dogs and went on the Tilt-A-Whirl over and over. It must have been some bad tamales."

Mr. Jiménez pushed his way through the crowd. "When exactly did you start to feel this way?"

"What are *you* doing here?" Nick growled, stepping between the man and his father.

The archaeologist ignored him. "Think. Did you begin feeling sick before your wife hit her head or after?"

Dad shivered as if he'd just had a bad chill. "I'm not sure. I wasn't sick when we went into the temple. I think it might have come on at about the same time."

Nick turned on Mr. Jiménez. "I told you to leave my parents alone." Carter and Angelo moved to his sides.

Mr. Jiménez shook his head. "This isn't possible."

Nick was about to tell the archaeologist he'd reveal the whole story, threats or not, when his mom suddenly sat up.

185

She looked around the crowd, her eyes so wide her pupils seemed to be lost in a sea of white. Slowly, she reached up and pulled off her bandages, revealing a nasty-looking bruise and at least a dozen stitches.

Nick stepped toward her, then froze as she held out her hands. Her palms glowed with a faint green luminescence.

"Mom?"

She stood, and the glow spread from her hands, up her arms, and over her entire body, like a shiny green cloud rising from her skin. She turned her head, and a pearly silver light shined on the crowd as if her eyes had been replaced by twin flashlights.

Mr. Jiménez stumbled backward, his jaw slack with terror. "No. This can't be. It's not possible. I'm the one who should have . . ."

Nick grabbed the man's sleeve, yanking him violently around. "What did you do to my mom?"

Mom raised her hands, and dark black clouds swirled above her head like a tornado. The crowd fell back, horrified.

"I. Have. Returned," Mom said. Only it wasn't her speaking. Her voiced sounded deep and powerful, like a monster or a . . .

"A god," Angelo whispered.

Mom grinned a fierce smile, baring all her teeth. Her face burned with such a bright green radiance that Nick had to squint to keep from being blinded by it. "It is I, Awilix of the Nija'ib' noble lineage. Goddess of the Moon. Queen of the Night."

There was an audible gasp from the people gathered before her. Several of the men turned and ran.

"Mom!" Nick cried. He turned to his father for help, but Dad was collapsed in his chair, his head thrown back and eyes closed.

Mom raised her hands, and twin bolts of lightning shot out from the clouds, striking the temples on both of the pyramids. "I go to gather my forces and reclaim my power," she roared, her voice like cracking thunder. "You'll all regret the day you disturbed our rest." With that she turned and began to climb the pyramid of the moon.

Carter watched her go, his mouth hanging open. He turned to Nick and grabbed his shoulder. "Dude, did you know she could do that?"

CHAPTER 19

ALGUIEN DEBE CUIDAR DE PAPÁ

SOMEONE NEEDS TO WATCH DAD

Nick stared at his mom's retreating figure. Except clearly she was no longer his mom. She'd turned into— what? Some kind of immortal being? He hurried to his father and tugged his hand. "Dad, wake up! Mom's in trouble."

Dad's eyes fluttered, and he mumbled something that sounded like *sick*, before passing out again.

"Dad, wake up!" Nick shouted. He hesitated, then slapped his father's face. How could he be sleeping at a time like this?

"He's not asleep," someone said behind Nick. He spun around to find Dr. Sofia Lopez, the librarian, standing behind him.

"What do you mean?" Nick shouted. "I need his help. Did you see my mom?"

Dr. Lopez nodded, her lips pressed tightly together. She searched through the crowd of people anxiously watching the glowing figure scale the pyramid of the moon. She grabbed one of the men by the shoulder and dragged him over. "Jiménez, what have you done?"

Mr. Jiménez blinked up at the librarian, who was a good six inches taller than him. He glanced nervously toward the boys. "I, um, don't know what you mean."

Dr. Lopez snatched his bag and pulled out the metal book. "I should have known. You were trying to steal the power of the gods."

"Not steal. Claim." He grabbed for the book, but she held it out of his grasp. "I am a direct descendant of the king. The power of Kinich Ahau should rightfully be mine." He stared in the direction of Nick's mom, who had nearly reached the top of the pyramid of the moon. "I don't understand what happened. Why did she get the power?"

Angelo, who had been silently watching everything, clapped a hand to his mouth. "The DNA test," he said, jabbing Jiménez in the chest with one finger. "What did you do with the paper I gave you?"

"What does that have to do with anything?" The

archaeologist reached into his pocket and pulled out the crumpled slip of paper.

Angelo snatched it from his hands and ran a finger down the numbers. "Of course. I thought something was off. But I was so focused on the matching pairs, I missed it completely."

"What does the DNA have to do with Nick's mom?" Carter asked.

Angelo slammed his hand against his forehead. "How could I have been so stupid? First I assumed that Dr. Canul was the one with the DNA match. Then I thought it was Jiménez. But the matching DNA sample wasn't from one of the men here in camp—it was from the control group. Your mom's DNA matches at least one of the DNA samples we found on the treasures in the underground room."

"What are you saying?" Nick asked, feeling dizzy. "My mom is . . ."

Angelo crushed the paper in his hand. "Mayan royalty. It's the only thing that makes sense. Jiménez is related to the uncle who isn't royal. Your mom must be a descendant of the aunt."

"Now just a minute," Mr. Jiménez said. "Of course my blood is royal. It's not even possible that—"

Carter cut off the archaeologist's pompous speech

with a punch to the jaw that dropped him to the ground. "That's for cursing my best friend's mom."

Jiménez wiped blood from his lip, but he didn't try to get back up. "How could *she* possibly have royal blood? She's an American."

Dr. Lopez turned to Nick. "Is there any chance your mother could have Mayan ancestors?"

Nick remembered the conversation he'd had with his mother in the kitchen just before they'd left on this trip. "I asked her how she knew Spanish, and she said her great-grandfather was from Mexico."

"That's it, then," Dr. Lopez said. "Your mother must be of royal lineage. She probably left some of her blood on the altar when she hit her head. When Jiménez performed the ceremony, it worked, but not on him."

"Glad you've got this all figured out," Nick snapped. "But how are you going to change her back from the moon goddess to my mom?"

"It's not that simple," Dr. Lopez said. "First, Awilix is not just the goddess of the moon. She is also the goddess of death, one of the most powerful goddesses in Mayan lore."

"The book wasn't specific on exactly which god's power was being summoned," Jiménez said. "I didn't really care as long as I got the power." He flinched when

191

Carter glared at him. "I'm sorry. I'm just trying to help."

Jiménez grabbed the book from Dr. Lopez and turned its metal pages until he came to a picture of a woman pulling a man out of a flaming pit. "Here. You must go to your mother, take her hand, and call her back from the dead. By now, she's already entered Xibalba. In order to get her back, you'll have to get past the lords of death."

"He's not going anywhere," Dr. Lopez said. "If anyone's going into Xibalba, it should be me."

Jiménez shook his head. "She can be brought back only by a blood relative."

Dr. Lopez shut the book. "It's too late to do anything tonight. But we'll begin searching first thing in the morning."

"That won't work," Jiménez said. "By morning the curse will be unbreakable. And your father won't last that long."

Nick's teeth clamped down so hard he bit his tongue. "What are you talking about?"

Jiménez sighed. "I told you, the ceremony requires a sacrifice. The life of an innocent—an outsider free of any Mayan heritage."

"That's why you brought us here," Angelo said. "You were going to sacrifice Nick."

Nick glared at the twisted little man. "You're saying my dad is the sacrifice? If we don't break the curse by morning, he'll die?"

Jiménez nodded. "I'm afraid so."

"Fine," Nick said. "How do I get to Xibalba?"

"Your mother went to the pyramid of the moon," Dr. Lopez said. "I say we start there."

Carter grabbed Mr. Jiménez's bag. "Where's that item of power you said you had?"

Angelo shook his head. "Whatever he thinks he found, it won't work. He was looking for something belonging to the king's uncle. We need an item that belonged to the king's aunt."

Jiménez sighed. "He's right. It will be something that meant a great deal to her. And possibly the child king as well. Unfortunately it will likely be with all the other treasures the king's aunt took to the underworld with her."

Nick closed his eyes. "So the item I need to guarantee safe passage past these demons is in a treasure room I can't get to without passing the demons."

"Sounds like my kind of challenge," Carter said. "When do we leave?"

"I'm going too," Angelo said. "The Three Monsterteers always stick together."

193

Dr. Lopez nodded. "Very well. I'll go with you."

Nick shook his head. "I need someone to watch my dad."

"I can't let you go alone," the librarian said. "Mr. Blackham would never forgive me if anything happened to you."

"You know Mr. Blackham?" Angelo asked.

Dr. Lopez blushed as if she wasn't supposed to give that way. "We've done business together from time to time. He knew I was in the area and asked me to keep an eye out for you."

A thought occurred to Nick. "You were the one who left the folder for us, weren't you?"

She nodded. "*Si.* I thought if you were going to be here you should at least know what you were getting into. Bartholomew warned me strange things might happen when you three showed up. But I was not expecting anything like this. *¡Cielos!*"

From the way she used Mr. Blackham's first name, Nick wondered if they were more than just coworkers. "Look," he said, "Mr. Blackham would want you to watch out for us. But he would also know that I can't save my mom unless I know my dad is okay. Besides, if anything happens to us, you're the only one who knows what Mr. Jiménez is really up to."

194

"Trust us," Carter said. "We've done this kind of thing before."

Dr. Lopez sighed. "All right. But be careful."

Nick bent over his dad and kissed him on the cheek. "Don't worry, I'll break the curse and bring Mom back."

CHAPTER 20

PODRÍA SEGUIR
JUGANDO ESTO
POR HORAS

I COULD PLAY THIS
FOR HOURS

By the time the boys reached the top of the pyramid, Nick's mother was gone, and the temple was empty.

"She must have gone through that dead end somehow," Angelo said as they slid the altar to the side, revealing the stone staircase below. "Let's hope she left it open behind her."

Walking down the stairs, Nick tried not to think about the dark stain on the side and top of the altar. Unfortunately, when they got to the end of the tunnel, it was blocked, just as it had been the first time they were here.

Angelo banged his hand on the cold stone wall. "That was a short trip."

"There has to be some way in," Nick said. "My mom found it. We can too."

Carter got down on one knee and studied the wall. "There's a hole here right under the picture of the moon. If we shove a couple of sticks of dynamite in, we can blow the whole wall."

"And probably bring the temple down on top of us," Angelo said.

"It doesn't matter anyway," Nick said. "We don't have any dynamite." He squatted down to look at the hole Carter had discovered. He pushed his finger into the hole but couldn't feel anything. "Maybe it takes some kind of key."

"Yes," Angelo said. "A key." He looked thoughtfully from the stair entrance to the door. "Of course!" he shouted, his face breaking into a smile. He ran to the mirror closest to the stairs. "Everybody stand back."

Slowly Angelo adjusted the mirror until it caught the light of the moon from outside. He moved to the second mirror, adjusting it until the moonlight bounced from the first mirror reflected into it. One by one he adjusted the mirrors, creating a continuous beam of silvery moonlight.

"Cross your fingers," he said, grabbing the last mirror. Carefully he moved the mirror until a single beam of light bounced from it straight into the hole in the wall. For a second, nothing happened. Then the wall began to move, and with a deep, grating sound it rumbled to the side until the entire entrance was open.

"We did it!" Carter said, pumping his fist.

Nick stepped through the open doorway and noticed several polished lengths of wood in a rack on the wall. "What are these?"

Angelo sniffed the wood. "*Pino de Ocote*. It's a fatwood pine that grows all around here. I think they're supposed to be used as torches."

"How are we supposed to light them?" Nick asked. He pulled a torch from the wall and it immediately burst into flame. "Well, that's convenient," he said.

"Maybe the demons want to make it easy to get to them so they can eat us," Carter said gloomily. He grabbed another length of wood and it lit as well. Soon all three of them were holding flaming torches.

"Let's take this slowly," Angelo said. "There could be any number of traps or tests here."

"Looks clear to me," Carter said. He held up his torch, revealing a wide, empty tunnel.

Nick couldn't help agreeing. If there was a trap, it sure wasn't in this tunnel. He started down the passage, but something moved in the dirt by his feet. He looked down just in time to see a gleaming white dome push up out of the ground. Another popped up from the ground in front of Carter, and two more to Angelo's left. All over the tunnel, gleaming white domes—about the size of cantaloupes—began rising from the ground.

"What are they?" Nick asked.

A second later, his question was answered, and he wished he'd never asked. Below the white domes, empty black eye sockets appeared next to champing teeth. The white things weren't cantaloupes. They were skulls—teeth opening and closing in silent chants. And the skulls were attached to skeleton bodies, covered with bits of tattered flesh and remnants of ancient Mayan clothing.

As soon as the nearest skeleton was out of the ground far enough to free its arms, it reached for Nick. Long, white bone fingers closed on the leg of his pants. "Get off me!" he screamed, waving his torch.

Dirt exploded into the air as dozens of skeletons dragged themselves out of the ground.

"Get back!" Angelo shouted, pulling Nick away from the clutching grasp of the sightless undead.

Carter turned and ran toward the stairs. "Retreat!"

Nick stood by the base of the stairs, panting. He could still feel the way the skeletal fingers had felt closing around his calf.

199

"I sure didn't expect that," Carter said. "You'd think they could put up a warning sign like *Caution, Skeletons Popping Up from the Floor*. They scared the beans out of me."

"I'm pretty sure that was on purpose," Angelo said.

The moment they'd all retreated past the entrance, the skeletons had sunk back into the ground. But Nick had no doubt they would climb out of their graves again if someone else trespassed into their tunnel.

"*Now* can we use dynamite?" Carter asked. "Even one of those hunting rifles would work." He held out his hands like he was gripping a rifle. "*Blam, blam. Blammety, blam.*"

"How would bullets kill skeletons?" Angelo asked.

"No clue," Carter said. "But if I was a skeleton and someone started shooting at me, I wouldn't stick around to find out."

Nick turned to Angelo. "How do we get past them?"

"What if we run?" Carter suggested. "It takes them a while to climb out of the ground. If we go fast, we can be past them before they can do anything but give us angry looks."

"How do we get back?" Angelo said.

Carter threw his hands in the air. "Do you expect

200

me to think of everything? I'll figure that out when it's time to come back."

It sounded chancy. But Nick didn't have any better ideas. "This is my problem. You guys wait here and I'll make a break for it. If I don't make it, maybe you can distract them or something."

"Who do you think you are, the Lone Ranger?" Carter said. "We're a team. Brothers from another mother. A creature-crunching crew."

"We might have a better chance if we stick together," Angelo said.

"Okay," Nick said. "Here's the plan. We line up at the door. I'll count to three, and then we all run. We're in this together, so if anyone gets grabbed, help them out." He took a deep breath. "One, two, three."

Either the skeletons were more prepared, having seen them once before, or they somehow guessed what the plan was. Nick hadn't taken more than three steps into the tunnel when undead began popping up like jack-in-the-boxes.

Two of them closed in on Nick, hands outstretched and teeth champing. Nick backed away, waving his torch in front of him. To his right, Angelo tried to kick away a skeleton that had its arms wrapped in a bear hug around his knees. He hit the creature across the arms with his torch and it released its grip just long enough for Angelo to get away.

"Back!" Nick shouted. He and Angelo hurried out of the tunnel.

But Carter was having fun. Waving his torch like a sword, he danced around the undead and shouted insults. "Is that the best you've got, bonehead!" he yelled, whacking a skeleton in the ribs. "My mom can fight better than that," he called, rolling across the ground and knocking one of the undead warrior's legs out from under it.

Nick turned to Angelo. "Was there anything in the *Popol Vuh* about these guys?"

Angelo flipped through his monster notebook. "Maybe there's a secret password or a special test." He glared at Carter, who was still fighting the skeletons. "Would you cut that out so I can think?"

"Just one more." Carter backed toward the doorway. He raised his torch in the air, yelled, "Die, you fleshless freak!" and bashed the skeleton directly on the top of its shiny white skull.

As soon as he hit it, the creature disappeared back into the ground.

"How did you do that?" Nick asked.

"I have no idea." Another skeleton moved in. Carter leaped forward and whacked it on top of the head. That one disappeared into the ground too. "It's like Whac-A-Mole with the undead," Carter chirped gleefully. "If only we got prizes."

Nick grinned at Angelo. "Anything about Whac-A-Mole in your Mayan studies?"

"Not a thing," Angelo said. He leaped forward and whapped a skeleton of his own. As soon as he hit the creature, it sank. He hit another, and the same thing happened.

Soon all three of them were bashing the undead into the ground. After a few seconds, the skeletons started to rise again, but they were much slower once they'd been hit.

"We can't just stand here bashing skeletons," Nick said. "We have to get my mom." When most of the skeletons were in the ground, he and his friends ran deeper into the tunnel. A hundred feet or so after the entrance, the tunnel turned sharply left and a steep staircase led down through a cave-like entrance into the heart of the pyramid.

"You think that was the only test?" Carter asked as the boys descended single file into the darkness, their torch light forming shadows on the carvings cut into the walls.

"It would be nice," Nick said. "But somehow I doubt it."

203

The deeper they went, the lower the temperature dropped, until Nick found himself shivering from the cold. The air smelled like the smoke from the torches, and something else. Something old and dark. Once again, he began to hear voices.

Turn back while you can.

Go away.

You don't belong here.

He decided it might be best to keep what he was hearing to himself.

The staircase continued farther than seemed possible. He felt like they'd been walking for half a mile at least. "Does it feel like we should have reached the bottom of the pyramid by now?"

Angelo's breath plumed in front of his face. "I don't think we're in the pyramid anymore. I think we're entering the underworld."

Carter shivered. "Do you really need to tell me that?"

At the bottom of the stairs, they found themselves standing in front of four doors—one to the left, one to the right, and two straight ahead. Each of the passages was a different color—red, black, white, and yellow.

Nick glanced down each of the passages. "Any suggestions?"

Angelo and Carter shook their heads.

"Okay, let's try white," he said.

Cautiously, the three boys filed down the passage. It went twenty or thirty feet before ending at an intersection that went left or right. A wet chewing sound came from the right.

"Left," Carter said. "Definitely left."

The passage curved around and then split into yet another fork.

"It's a maze," Angelo said.

Nick agreed. "Is anybody keeping track of this?"

"I'm trying." Angelo scratched something into his monster notebook. "It's hard to draw a map without an aerial view."

"Let's go right this time," Carter said. "I've got a good feeling about it." A minute later they came out back at the stairs where they'd started.

"How did we end up here?" Nick asked.

Carter shrugged. "Maybe we should have gone left the second time?"

Nick pointed to the door on the right. "Let's start with that one."

Again, they found themselves taking lefts and rights with no idea where they were. Once, Nick was sure he heard quiet voices to their left. But when they turned that direction, they again found themselves exactly where they'd started.

205

"Hang on," Angelo said. "Something about these colors seems familiar." He flipped through his monster notebook. "Here it is. In the *Popol Vuh*, the brothers had to choose one of four roads. They were red, black, white, and yellow, just like these."

"Which one did they choose?" Nick asked.

Angelo examined the pages. "I should have taken better notes, but I didn't think I'd need them. Black, maybe? I think that's the color that took them to the lords of death."

"Very comforting," Carter said.

"It's still a maze though," Nick said. "Even after we take the black path, we have to figure out a way to leave a trail so we can tell where we've gone."

Angelo tried burning a spot on the wall with his torch, but the fire left no mark. He tried scraping the wall with the wood. That didn't work either. "We could drop rocks."

Carter pointed to the ground, which was as clean as the floor of a restaurant kitchen. "Have you seen any rocks in here?"

Nick hadn't. "What about your yarn? That would work great."

"Jiménez took it when he knocked me out." Carter sighed. "And the hat I was working on too."

206

"I had lots of stuff in my backpack," Angelo said. "But he took that too."

The three of them looked around for something to drop. Without a way to mark their path, they could end up wandering through the labyrinth for hours.

"You know . . . ," Angelo said.

Nick followed his gaze and realized what he was thinking. Both of the boys looked at Carter with a combination of eagerness and pity.

"What?" Carter asked.

Nick pointed to a loose piece of yarn hanging from the bottom of Carter's serape.

"No!" Carter said. "Do you have any idea how hard this was to make? I love it like a brother."

"It's the only way," Nick said.

Carter bit his lip. "Do you have any idea what you're asking?"

Nick patted him on the shoulder. "We don't have to use all of it."

Carter hugged the serape to his chest. "That's like saying, 'We don't have to cut off all your fingers.'"

"It's for Nick's mom," Angelo said.

Carter grimaced. "Fine." He closed his eyes, grabbed the threaded end of the yarn, and tugged.

207

CHAPTER 21

LLORÉ AL VER
OLD YELLER

I CRIED DURING
OLD YELLER

"It's okay, little fellah," Carter said, petting his serape.

Nick looked at Angelo, and they both raised their eyebrows at the same time. Nick had no idea how long they'd been down here. All he knew was that so far, Carter had unraveled almost a third of the yarn from the front of his serape, and they'd walked so long Nick's feet were getting blisters.

They hadn't managed to find their way through the maze. But at least thanks to the yarn they hadn't ended up back where they started. Now they reached a dead end—one of at least a dozen they'd been blocked by so far. Carter patted what was left of his serape. "Daddy still loves you."

"You know, it's just a piece of clothing," Angelo said as they doubled back.

"*Seriously?*" Carter glared at him. "If your friend's cat died, would you say, 'It's just an animal'? When Travis had to shoot Old Yeller, did his mom say, 'Stop blubbering. It's only a dog'?"

Angelo looked away. "Sorry."

"Point taken," Nick said. "We really appreciate the sacrifice you're making. And if it helps, I promise I'll buy you like twenty packages of yarn if we make it out of this."

"Skeins," Carter muttered. "Yarn comes in balls and skeins."

"Fine. I'll buy you twenty *skeins* of yarn."

"Look," Angelo said. "It's a door."

Nick could barely believe his eyes. After all this time, he'd started to wonder if there even *was* a way out of the maze. The thought had crossed his mind that this was just a trap where they'd wander aimlessly until they died of thirst or starvation.

They hurried to the door, which was covered from top to bottom in Mayan script.

"What does it say?" Nick asked.

Angelo squinted at the carvings and shook his head. "I'm not sure. I should have spent more time studying Mayan before we left."

"Only one way to find out," Nick said. He pushed the heavy stone door and all their torches went out at once.

"What happened?" Nick asked. *Appened-appened-appened*, his voice echoed, as if they had entered a large cavern. Had they gone through the door then, or were they still in the maze? He reached out but couldn't feel anything. It was so dark that even when he waved his hand in front of his face he couldn't see so much as a shadow of movement.

"No clue," Carter said. "But I'm going to take a wild guess here and assume the writing on the door said something about darkness."

"Didn't you say something about darkness being one of the tests in that book?" Nick asked.

"Yes. The house of darkness," Angelo said.

That didn't sound too bad. Nick didn't exactly like the dark, and he had to admit he felt a little freaked out about having no idea where he was or what might be waiting for him. But he could live with that.

"Now isn't the time to panic," Angelo said. "Although I think this is where the first set of brothers died."

"Died!" Carter yelped. "How did they die?"

Angelo coughed. "I . . . don't remember. I know

210

there was a house of darkness, and four or five others. A house of blades maybe?"

"*Blades*," Carter said. "Now is definitely the time to panic."

"We can get through this." Nick moved in the direction Carter's voice had come from, his hand held out in front of him.

Carter squealed. "Something touched me!"

"It's just me," Nick said. "Put your hand on my shoulder."

Carter poked him in the face.

"I didn't say pick my nose," Nick said, moving Carter's hand to his shoulder.

"Now, Angelo, walk toward the sound of my voice." A moment later something bumped into his chest, and he barely kept from screaming.

He turned Angelo in the direction he thought was forward and placed his hands on his friend's shoulders. "Okay, Angelo, you lead the way. One step at a time. Shuffle your feet and hold your hands in front of you. There could be pits or walls. If you start to fall or run into anything, yell and I'll pull you back. Carter, you hold on to me, and keep feeding out your yarn."

"What if something grabs me from behind?" Carter asked.

"Scream like a little girl and hope it goes away."

Step by step, the three of them moved through the darkness. Nick tried to keep cool, but with nothing to see or feel, every little sound made him sure something was about to grab him.

"Do you feel anything?" Carter called from the back.

"Only your hand digging into my shoulder blade," Nick said.

Carter snorted. "Well, excuse me for not wanting to get separated."

Angelo stopped suddenly and Nick banged into his back. "There's something here. It feels like . . ." There was a wet squelching sound, and Angelo backed away. "Disgusting. It's all squishy."

"Taste it," Carter said. "It might be Jell-O."

"It's not Jell-O." Angelo sounded slightly nauseated. "And I'm not tasting it. It smells like pig guts."

Nick felt his stomach roll over.

They moved around the squishy stuff and walked for several minutes in silence. Suddenly Angelo cried out, "I'm falling!"

Nick felt his friend tilt forward and pulled back with all his strength. For a second, Angelo continued to lean, and Nick felt his fingers slipping. He yanked as hard as he could and Angelo fell backward against him. His breathing sounded loud and harsh in the darkness. "What was it?" Nick asked.

"Some kind of drop-off," Angelo gasped. Nick felt Angelo kneel down, and a moment later he said, "I can't feel the bottom."

"We can't keep going like this or one of us is going to get killed," Nick said. "If only we had some light."

"Hey," Carter called. "I feel something."

"You feel *me*," Nick said.

"No. Right after you said we need light, something bumped my foot. It felt kind of like . . ." There was a shuffling sound, and suddenly a flame lit the darkness. "It's another torch," Carter said, holding the flaming stick over his head. "Look, there's a pile of them right here."

Angelo's face went pale. "Put it out!" he yelled, grabbing the torch from Carter's hand and stubbing out the flames on the ground.

"Are you crazy?" Nick shouted. "What did you do that for?"

"Hang on," Carter said. "I'll get another one."

"No." Angelo sounded terrified. "I remember now. When the first two brothers went into the house of darkness, the lords of death gave them sticks to burn.

They told them they had to return the sticks uncharred, but the brothers used them to light the darkness. That's why they cut off one of their heads."

Carter's gulp was so loud, Nick could hear it in the darkness.

"That book of yours didn't happen to say how to get through this place, did it?" Nick asked.

"I'm sure it did," Angelo said. "But I didn't put it in my . . ." He snapped his fingers, the sound clear and sharp in the darkness. "My notes. That's it!" There was a crinkling sound in the darkness.

"What are you doing?" Nick asked.

The crinkling sound came again. "Okay, when I say now, light another torch. Then put it right back out. Now!"

Nick heard Carter moving around, and a torch burst into flame. Angelo shoved something into the fire and yelled, "Put it out! Put it out!"

Carter smashed the torch into the ground, but this time the room didn't go dark. Angelo held something that guttered brightly over his head. It took Nick a second to realize what Angelo was burning. It was a page from his monster notebook. "Dude, you can't do that!" he yelled. "That means more to you than anything."

As the flames reached the bottom of the paper,

Angelo tore another page from his notebook and dropped the smoldering remains of the first page. "If Carter can unravel his serape to help us, I can burn some of my notes," he said. "Come on, let's get out of here before I get to the Mayan section."

Stopping and starting with each new burning page, like a bizarre game of Red Light Green Light, they at last found a door. Nick grabbed the handle, and the door swung open with a metallic squeal. Gray light blinded them all.

"We made it," Nick said, stumbling forward. He blinked his eyes, trying to adjust to the sudden brightness.

"Hang on," Angelo said. "This could be another one of the tests."

"It doesn't feel cold. What if it's the blade room?" Carter asked.

"Don't get cut," Nick said. It was the only advice he could think of.

Slowly their surroundings came into focus. They seemed to be in a cavern of some kind. The ceiling was hidden in darkness and the ground was covered in leaves and twigs, all coated with a powdery white substance. The air was filled with the strong stink of ammonia.

Nick shrugged. "Other than the smell, this isn't too bad."

215

Angelo frowned. "That's what I'm afraid of." He knelt to the ground, touched the white powder, and sniffed his fingers. He dropped his hand with a jerk, stood, and looked up with an expression of alarm. "I think we're in the bat room."

CHAPTER 22

NO SÉ CUALES SON PEORES, LOS MURCIÉLAGOS, O LOS GATOS

I'M NOT SURE WHICH IS WORSE, BATS OR CATS

"The bathroom?" Carter laughed. "What's so scary about a bathroom?"

"Not bath," Angelo said. "*Bat*. As in the killer kind."

From overhead came a pounding of wings. All at once, a huge black cloud raced down at them. "Get out of here!" Angelo yelled.

With no idea where he was going, Nick broke into a sprint. Something sharp clawed at the back of his scalp, and he looked back to see thousands of bats diving toward him.

"That way!" Angelo yelled, pointing toward a rock that curved over to form a small shelter under the bottom of it. The three boys dove under the rock, pushing handfuls of leaves and sticks into the opening to keep the bats from getting in.

It was a tight squeeze, and Nick could feel sweat start to form on his head.

"Well, that was interesting," Carter said. "Honestly, it looked a lot cooler in the Batman movies."

"Tell me the *Popol Vuh* has something for this situation," Nick said. With the three boys jammed side to side it was already getting hot and stuffy. He didn't know how long they could stay here.

Angelo coughed. "Actually, this room didn't end up so well. Even for the second set of brothers who made it through. They hid for a while. But eventually one of them stuck out his head and the bats cut it off and took it to the lords of death. His brother replaced his head with a turtle until they could get the real one back."

"Please tell me you're kidding," Nick said.

"Sorry," Angelo muttered.

Nick wiped a hand across his face. "Let's think of something better than that."

"Hang on," Carter said. "I have an idea." He started squirming around, which was difficult for everyone.

"Careful," Angelo said. "You're jabbing me in the ribs."

"Would you rather have a turtle for a head?" Carter

continued to poke and move until Nick was about to go crazy. But at last he handed something to Nick. "What do you think?"

In the almost complete darkness, Nick could see only what looked like a small basketball. It felt sharp and prickly.

"I made it out of leaves and twigs," Carter said.

Nick appreciated the effort but wasn't sure what they were going to do with a big ball of leaves. "It's, um, nice."

"Don't you get it?" Carter asked. "It's a fake head. One of us pulls our shirt up over our head, holds the ball against his collar, and when the bats take the bait, we make a break for it."

"Sounds great," Angelo said. "Until they realize it's a fake and rip off the real thing."

Nick thought it through. He remembered reading something in science class about how bats didn't have good eyesight. Instead they used sonar—or was it radar? "I'll do it," he said.

"Are you sure?" Angelo rolled onto his side to face him. "There are a lot of bats out there with sharp teeth and claws."

"We can't stay in here forever," Nick said. "You guys have some serious body-odor issues. Besides, you burned pages from your monster notebook and Carter unraveled his serape. What's my head compared to that?"

He pulled his shirt up over his head, accidentally bopping Angelo in the eye.

"Scream really loud when they pull it off," Carter said. "So they think it's really your head."

"If they pulled off his head, he wouldn't be able to scream," Angelo said, and Nick could practically hear him rolling his eyes.

Carter grunted. "They don't know that."

Nick pushed the leaf ball against the top of his head and wormed his way out. For a moment, nothing happened, and he wondered whether the bats were still there. Maybe he could take a quick peek. Then something that felt more like an eagle than a bat ripped the ball from his grasp.

"Are you still alive?" Carter asked.

"I think so," Nick said. Slowly, he peeked out from the top of his shirt. The bats were gone. "It worked!" he shouted, climbing out of the hole. Carter and Angelo quickly followed him.

With the bats roosting back on the ceiling, it was easy to see the next door on the other side of the cavern. "Any idea what's through there?" Nick asked.

220

Angelo checked his notes. "Let's see. Lords of death. Roads. Maybe I wrote something in the back of—"

"Guys," Carter interrupted. "I think we might have a problem." He pointed toward the ceiling, where the bats were beginning to flutter around again. Suddenly a dark sphere dropped from the air and exploded on the ground. "I think they just figured out the head is a fake."

Like a great black glove, the bats flew from the ceiling and straight at the boys.

"Run for the door!" Nick yelled.

"Run for your lives!" Carter echoed.

The cloud of bats was nearly on top of them as they reached the other side of the room. With no time to worry about what was on the other side, Nick yanked open the door and slammed it shut as soon as his friends were through.

Trying to catch their breath, the three of them looked around. They were standing in a small, round room with a pit in the center. On the other side of the room was another door. But standing between them and the door was a powerful-looking black-spotted jaguar.

The big cat stretched its limber body and bared a mouthful of razor-sharp teeth. "Welcome to the house of the jaguar."

All three boys stared silently at the green-eyed predator.

"Cat got your tongue?" the jaguar asked, flashing what looked to Nick like a grin.

Carter was the first to speak. "We hate to bother you. It's just that, um, Nick's mom turned into a, uh . . . And we need to, well . . ." He edged left, and the big cat moved to block him.

"I know what you seek." The jaguar swished its tail toward the door behind it. "It's right through there. And I'll be happy to let you pass. For a price."

Nick tried to swallow, but his throat was so dry, his Adam's apple refused to move. "What price?"

The jaguar lunged toward them, snarling when the boys fell back against the wall. "There are three of you, and only one of me. But I'm dreadfully hungry. I can't remember the last good meal I've had. Let's strike a bargain. Let me eat one of you, and I'll let the other two through the door. Or refuse, and I'll eat all of you."

Nick pressed against the back of the room, his hands slick with sweat on the wall. Even if they'd been armed, they might not have been able to kill the jaguar before it reached them. With no weapons they didn't stand a chance.

He glanced at Angelo, who looked as terrified as he

was. There didn't seem to be any way out of this.

Carter rubbed his chin. "Let me make sure I understand. We feed you, and you let us go?"

"That's right," the jaguar snarled. "But decide quickly or I'll eat you all."

"I've already decided," Carter said. "I'm the smallest of the three of us. So you don't want me."

"What are you doing?" Nick whispered.

The jaguar licked its chops. "Go on."

Carter moved back to his right. "And Nick is too bony. Which leaves only one choice. Something big, a little crunchy, and filling."

Angelo stared at Carter. "If this is about me making fun of your serape . . ."

"An excellent choice," the jaguar said. It bunched its haunches and prepared to leap.

"No!" Nick cried.

At the same second the cat jumped, Carter reached behind him and yanked open the door. Clouds of small black bats flew through the opening and into the jaguar's mouth. The cat coughed, spat, and clawed, but the bats smothered it in a thick black cloud.

"I'm fresh out of bones, but how about a thick, juicy bat sandwich!" Carter yelled, and the three of them ran across the room and out the last door.

223

Nick clapped Carter on the back. "Dude, that was the coolest thing ever. I totally thought you were going to feed Angelo to the jaguar."

They were back in the maze again—their torches once more burning—but for the moment, Nick didn't even care. He was just glad they hadn't been eaten. "Didn't you think so too, Angelo?" he asked. "You should have seen yourself."

Even though they had escaped the jaws of the cat, Angelo's face was still drawn.

"What's wrong?" Nick asked.

Angelo pointed ahead, through an archway Nick hadn't noticed the first time, if, in fact, it had been there at all. On the other side of the arch, two figures stood on polished stone pedestals. "I'm pretty sure those are the lords of death."

CHAPTER 23

¡QUE...
ASCO ES ESTO!

THIS IS JUST...
DISGUSTING!

The first figure was dressed all in black. A tight-fitting cloak covered him from head to foot. The front of the cloak appeared to be made of clawed pincers snapping open and shut across his chest. The bottom of his cloak moved around him with a life of its own, and Nick realized it was made of squirming black centipedes.

His face was a bone-white skull, and Nick couldn't tell whether it was a mask or not. The skull turned to the boys and spoke. "I am Hun-Came, One Death."

The second figure was clad only in a fur loincloth and a feathered mask. Bits of bone seemed to have been thrust through the flesh of his arms, legs, and chest. As Nick watched, he split into two figures, then three, four, five, six, and finally seven.

Each of the seven figures wore a different mask—each made to look like a bloodthirsty beast. Each held a different weapon, ranging from swords to spears to long, curved knives and stone axes. The men all raised their weapons over their heads and spoke as one, "I am Vucub-Came, Seven Death. The living do not belong in Xibalba. Tell me why you trespass here before we make you one of our own."

Nick stepped up to the archway, legs trembling. "I'm, um, Nick Braithwaite." He gave a little wave and felt dumb when the men only continued to stare at him. "The thing is, my mom got turned into this, uh, god."

"Awilix," Angelo whispered.

"Right, Awilix. Anyway, I need to find her and break the curse."

"You seek Awilix's chamber?" One Death asked.

Nick nodded. "Yeah, she's my mom."

All the copies of Seven Death looked at one another and seemed to reach a conclusion. "You may enter."

Nick breathed a sigh of relief. He started forward with Carter and Angelo.

"But," One Death shouted, "know that you must first pass by the ten demons—paying a penance to each. Should you fail, you and your friends will be thrust from Xibalba forever."

Carter stepped forward. "Um, can I get some clarification on the second part? What exactly do you mean by 'paying a penance'?"

"The ten demons may torture you as they will. But they may not kill you."

"Okay," Carter said. "Well, I guess that's kind of good news."

Nick turned to his friends. "Look, I appreciate you guys coming this far. But I will totally understand if you want to wait here."

"I've been lost, attacked by bats, and nearly fed to a jaguar," Carter said. "What's a little torture compared to that?"

Angelo stepped quickly forward and grabbed One Death's hand. "It's a deal."

The lord of death yanked his hand away in surprise. "Mortals may not touch the lords!" he shouted. Instantly, the figures disappeared and the three boys found themselves in a long passageway. Looking back, Nick could still see the maze beyond the arch, but it was slightly distorted, as though he were seeing it through a thick pane of glass.

He started down the passage and noticed a pair of alcoves set in each side of the hallway. As he reached the openings, two winged creatures flew down from black onyx pedestals. They were, by far, the most disgusting creatures he'd ever seen. The one on the left looked like someone had been at it with a sanding machine. Open wounds covered its crusty red body and scaly wings. The one on the right was made of dripping, red-black goo.

"We are the demons of sick blood," the demons shouted in wet gurgling voices.

Suddenly Nick felt as though his entire body was on fire. Pain racked his muscles and doubled him over.

"Ahh!" Angelo screamed, clutching his stomach.

"It hurts so bad," Carter bellowed, his face bright red. "Make it stop."

Nick dropped to his knees. The pain was horrendous. "How . . . did . . . the brothers . . . ," he gasped. He couldn't say any more. It felt like he was going to faint.

Angelo's mouth dropped open and he clawed through the pages of his monster notebook. "You are Xiquiripat, the Flying Scab," he called to the one on the left. "And you are Cuchumaquic, Gathered Blood."

Instantly the demons disappeared.

Nick stood up slowly. The pain was gone, but he still felt like he'd just finished three rounds with a black belt. "How did you make them go away?" he finally managed to ask.

"I named them," Angelo said. "When you speak their names, they have no power over you."

Carter rubbed his stomach. "No offense, but next time how about you say the names a little quicker."

Nick agreed. He wasn't sure he could make it through four more pairs of demons like this.

At the next set of openings, two more demons flew down to meet him. The first was covered in weeping sores, and the other had a strange yellowish tint to its bulbous body.

"We are they who cause mortals' bodies to swell up," the demons announced.

As soon as they spoke the words, Nick's body seemed to double in weight. His hands turned into balloons and his head felt like it was the size of a pumpkin.

"Can't breathe," Angelo said, clutching his chest.

Carter, who looked like a badly-out-of-shape Oompa-Loompa, turned to Angelo and grunted. "Say their names before I have a heart attack."

"Ahalpuh, Pus Demon, and Ahalgana, Jaundice Demon," Angelo panted.

The demons disappeared.

Nick tried to catch his breath. His legs felt wobbly. But he had to keep going.

The next two demons were nothing but bones with ragged bits of flesh hanging off.

"We eat the flesh from your bones until your life is gone," the demons said, and Nick suddenly felt weak.

His arms and legs were quickly turning into sticks, the muscles and fat seeming to melt away like wax. He turned to see Carter's face shrivel like an old woman's.

"Name them," Carter screeched in a voice that sounded nothing like him.

"Chamiabac, Bone Staff," Angelo wheezed like a dying old man. "And Chamiaholom, Skull Staff."

Nick stumbled forward and nearly fell. "Let's get this over with," he said. "I can't take much more."

"I feel like I got sucked through a vacuum cleaner and spit out through the dust bag," Carter croaked.

The boys limped down the hall. At the next intersection, two ancient-looking hags flew down to meet them. The one on the left held what looked like a witch's broom, while the one on the right clutched a knife nearly long enough to be called a sword.

The hags cackled. "We hide in the unswept areas of people's houses and stab them to death."

Almost before Nick felt a searing pain in his gut, Angelo shouted, "Ahalmez, the Sweepings Demon, and Ahaltocob, the Stabbing Demon."

"Good one," Nick said.

Angelo nodded weakly. "Only two more to go."

"Look," Carter said, pointing to the end of the tunnel.

The end of the passage seemed to be covered by some kind of hazy mist, but Nick thought he could just make out a room filled with treasures. A figure lay on a bed in the middle.

"I think that's your mom," Carter said.

Nick felt a burst of new energy. "Let's get this done." He patted Angelo on the shoulder. "You know, you may have been wrong about the aliens. But we couldn't have made it this far without your research. Whatever kind of scientist you end up being, you're gonna be a good one."

"Thanks," Angelo said. "Whatever my parents think, that means a lot."

The last two demons were so small, Nick nearly missed them when they glided down from their pedestals. Their bright red bodies were no bigger than newborn babies—although their sharp horns and bony wings made it clear they were anything but human.

"Let me have it," Nick said. "Let's get this over with."

The tiny demons looked at each other with something like amusement. "We're not nearly as powerful as our brothers. In fact, we really don't hurt much at all. As long as you don't mind dying by coughing up blood."

As soon as the word *blood* left the demons' mouths, Nick felt a gush of liquid heat burst from his nose. Dark red liquid splashed on his shirt and pants. It was the worst nosebleed he'd ever had. His nostrils were running like a faucet.

231

Beside him, Angelo gave a great hacking cough.

"Name them," Carter called. His voice was muffled and Nick saw red seeping through the fingers he had plastered over his mouth.

"I can't," Angelo gagged.

"What do you mean you can't?" Nick turned to find Angelo staring at his monster notebook in horror. The page was covered with red. Angelo tried to wipe it away with the palm of his hand. But he coughed again and more blood gushed down on the paper, so thick the words underneath were unreadable.

Nick's head began to sway. He looked at the floor and couldn't believe how much blood there was. Had that all come from him? "Got. To. Try," he whispered. The hallway was spinning around him.

Distantly, he heard Angelo try to speak. But the blood was too thick in his throat. All he managed to do was cough out something that sounded like *grok*.

"Wrong!" the demons sang together. "You lose."

Suddenly the blood vanished, and Seven Death appeared before them, raising his arms. "You have chosen the false path and are forever banned from Xibalba."

CHAPTER 24

AÚN SIN
PANTALONES,
UN GUERRERO
SIEMPRE ES
UN GUERRERO

EVEN WITH NO
PANTS, A WARRIOR
IS A WARRIOR

Nick pounded on the wall. "I have to get back in there."

"I'm so sorry," Angelo said. "I blew it."

After Angelo had said the wrong name, One Death had returned them to the tunnel under the temple of the moon. But this time, no matter what they did with the mirrors, the door refused to open.

Nick turned around and punched his fist against a mirror, the metal ringing like a gong in the enclosed space. "We were so close. How could I have let us fail?"

"It's not your fault, either of you," Carter said. "Even if you'd remembered the name, there was no way to say it with your mouth full of blood. The whole thing was rigged. We'll just have to find another way in."

"There is no other way," Angelo said. "We failed. I failed."

Nick dropped to the ground and put his head in his hands. According to his watch, dawn was only an hour or two away. With it, his mother would be a monster forever, and his dad . . . He couldn't even think about that.

"Maybe you could ask the ghosts that were talking to you before for some advice," Carter suggested.

Nick looked up. "What did you say?"

"It's not like the ghosts are going to tell you how to get in," Angelo said.

Nick jumped to his feet. "Maybe they did. It says *Death is the beginning* on the door, and that's the same thing I heard one of the voices say."

"The beginning of a lot of trouble from what I can see," Carter said.

"Shhh." Nick held his finger up to his lips. He had to think. "The entrance to the underground says *Death is the beginning*. The beginning of what?"

"The path to Xibalba, I assume," Angelo said.

"Right. The path my mom's on right now. Which means I have to follow that same path."

"Dude." Carter grabbed him by the arm. "Are you saying what I think you're saying?"

"Huh?" Nick had no idea what Carter was talking about.

"You can't kill yourself," Carter said. "No matter how bad things look."

"Who said anything about killing myself?" Nick turned to Angelo. "Dr. Lopez said the Mayans believed there were three kinds of entrances to the underworld. Caves, tunnels, and . . ."

"Pools," Angelo said.

"Exactly. The entrance from this pyramid was a cave leading to a tunnel. But what about the pyramid of the sun? How would they get to the underworld?"

Carter's eyes lit up. "The pool with the waterfall we saw the first night!"

Nick pounded him on the shoulder. "Exactly. I saw a carving in that pyramid, and the voices there said something about the river of the dead. I'd bet anything that pool is connected to it. To get to my mom, all I have to do is dive into the pool and swim down the river of the dead."

"This could be a problem," Angelo said.

After sneaking down from the pyramid of the moon and past the camp, the three of them were crouched at the top of the pyramid of the sun. But between them

235

and the temple with the entrance to the pyramid was an army of creatures that would give anyone nightmares for years. Not to mention some serious counseling bills.

There were at least three or four dozen skeletons, marching around and around the temple. They were wearing ragged pieces of metal and leather armor, and helmets with the remains of moldy feathers sticking out of the top. Even worse, they were all armed with wicked-looking spears.

Closer to the temple, there were eight or ten mummies. Nick thought they must have been executioners when they were alive, because each of them carried an ax Nick wasn't even sure he'd be able to lift. They didn't appear to be as fast as the skeletons. But they were clearly much stronger.

Finally, several shadowy shapes were prowling around just inside the temple. Nick couldn't see what they were. But they definitely weren't anything good.

"Maybe I can sneak by them," Nick whispered. It was still dark, but it wouldn't be for long.

"Not a chance," Angelo said. "Even with all the men in camp on our side, I don't think we could fight our way through this army. Someone doesn't want you inside."

"I have to try," Nick said. "Wouldn't you guys if it was your mom?"

236

"I've got an idea," Carter said. "Angelo, come with me. Nick, wait here until our signal, then run to the temple as fast as you can."

"What's your signal?" Nick asked.

Carter winked. "You'll know it when you see it."

Carter and Angelo dropped down a few steps and hurried around the north side of the pyramid. Nick peeked over the eastern hills. How long would it be before the sun came up?

Trying to calm his nerves, he began to count by twos. "Two, four, six . . ." What was Carter's plan? It wouldn't be something crazy like dynamite, would it? Although now that he thought about it, he wished they actually had dynamite. Because that would definitely do some damage.

"Fourteen, sixteen, eighteen . . ." What if they panicked and took off? He could wait here until the sun came up, never realizing that there would be no signal. That was nuts. His friends would never abandon him.

He was up to 180, and thinking about going on his own, when a bloodcurdling scream split the air. Angelo jumped up from the east side of the pyramid and ran straight past the temple. Nick blinked, unable to believe what he was seeing. Angelo was waving his hands in the air, and he was wearing only his boxers.

"Awilix stole my clothes!" he screamed. "Somebody help me. The moon goddess is a clothes thief!"

Nick shook his head. This was an even crazier plan than dynamite.

But it seemed to be working. The skeletons and mummies immediately broke ranks and began to chase after Angelo, who zigzagged back and forth across the pyramid, drawing them farther and farther away from the temple.

At the same time, Carter jumped up from the north side of the pyramid and yelled at a nearby skeleton warrior, "Hey, you, your femur is showing!"

The guards that hadn't chased after Angelo started toward Carter. Carter froze in place, and for a panicked moment, Nick thought they were going to catch him. At the last minute, Carter sprinted to his left and looped around the skeletons and mummies. He ran a complete circle around them, then started another.

Nick couldn't understand what he was doing until one of the skeletons suddenly tripped and fell. Carter tightened his circle and another skeleton collided with a mummy.

Nick burst into surprised laughter. It was the yarn. Carter was wrapping the guards with layer after layer of yarn. Suddenly he realized the way was clear to the temple. Leaping to his feet, he raced across the top of the pyramid. A few of the guards spotted him halfway to the temple. But they were too late. He'd reach the entrance well before they did.

Sprinting like a halfback heading for the end zone, he charged around the temple and into the entrance. He was almost to the wall that opened into the underground passage when a pair of four-legged shapes slipped out of the shadows.

Nick skidded to a halt. Jaguars. "Good kitties," he said softly, trying to edge around them. But the cats weren't having any of it. They closed in on him from both sides. Where could he go? It was too late to turn back, and he couldn't get past them to the underground entrance.

The only thing he could think of was pictures he'd seen of jaguars curled at the feet of Mayan kings. Holding out his hand and trying to keep his voice from trembling, he said, "I am of royal blood, and I command you to let me pass."

It wasn't working. The jaguars snarled and started toward him. He thought about saying he was the son of Awilix. But he couldn't. Even though the Queen of the Night might have his mother's body, she wasn't his mom.

Instead, he tried shouting one more time, with as much authority as he could, "My mother is a direct descendant of your queen, and I am her son. In the name of my great-whatever grandmother, I command you to let me pass."

Amazingly, it worked. The jaguars turned and stalked off. He didn't have any time to celebrate though, because just then Carter shouted, "Hurry! They're coming."

Nick ran to the wall. He pushed on the tooth in the floor, shot though the doorway before it was completely open, and pushed the rock closed again. As the door slammed in place, he realized he'd forgotten to bring a light. He might be inside, but he couldn't see a thing.

CHAPTER 25

PERDÓNAME SI LLORO UN POQUITO

EXCUSE ME IF I CRY A LITTLE

Now that he was inside, the question was how to get down to the pool. He tried to remember the way they'd gone the first time. But that night was mostly a blur. All he could remember was the voices asking if it was time.

Knowing he was going too slow, he held his hands out in front of him and took one step, then another. Something brushed against his foot and gave a metallic *clink*. He reached down and felt something soft and round. Carter's yarn ball and needles. Jiménez must have hidden them here when Nick and his friends were unconscious.

Nick didn't have any use for yarn. But if Carter's things were here . . . He knelt on the floor, feeling around until his fingers brushed against the smooth nylon of a backpack. Quickly he unzipped the pockets and felt around inside. His hand closed on a metal cylinder. He pulled it out and pushed the button, and blessed light filled the tunnel.

With no time to lose, he raced along the hallway. Now it was all coming back to him. He turned down the staircase and leaped the steps three or four at a time, ducking his head to keep from hitting it on the low ceiling. Soon he could hear the rushing of water. He listened to see if he could hear any voices, but no one was speaking to Nick tonight.

Reaching the bottom of the stairs, he turned the corner and ran to the pool. He started to pull off his shirt, and the beam of his light hit the water. Something was moving there. He stepped closer and then jerked back in horror.

Scorpions. The pool was filled with huge scorpions—long, sharp stingers pointing out from their tails. That was impossible. Scorpions lived in the desert, not in the water. Angelo had said something about a river of scorpions. But had that been real or imaginary? He put the toe of his shoe near the water and a scorpion clattered over to it and plunged its stinger into the rubber sole. It felt real enough.

He tried to remember everything Angelo had told him about the *Popol Vuh*. The one thing all the tests seemed to have in common was that they were tricks—tests of will more than anything else. The demons hadn't really made them bleed or swell up or lose their flesh. He just had to hope this test would be the same.

"Doesn't matter if it's real or not," he said. After everything he'd been through, he wasn't going to let this stop him. If they were imaginary, he'd be fine. If they were real, then, well, they'd just have to sting him. Quickly he stripped off his shoes, pants, and shirt.

He hoped the flashlight would work in the water. Again, if it didn't, he'd figure something out. He inhaled deeply, sucking as much air into his lungs as possible. He didn't know how long he'd have to be underwater. A scorpion climbed up onto the bank, and he kicked it back into the pool with the side of his bare foot—narrowly avoiding the stinger.

Another deep breath. Exhale. Inhale. Filling his lungs until he thought they would burst, he put his hands over his head and dove into the pool of churning scorpions. Instantly, the water grabbed him and pulled him down. He opened his eyes, but he couldn't see anything except bubbles. The pull of the current grew stronger. Now he was going not just down, but sideways as well.

In the beam of his light, he saw a rocky outcropping coming directly toward him. He pushed off to keep from hitting his head and somersaulted into the current. Now he was out of control, rocks scraping his arms, back, and shoulders. He tried to figure out which way was up, but the river was too deep—the current too strong.

His chest began to burn and he blew some air out of his nose. How long had he been down here? He released another burst of used oxygen and his brain demanded he breathe. It was everything he could do not to open his mouth and suck in, the way his lungs were ordering him to. Just as he was about to gray out, the river tossed him to the surface. He coughed and gasped as oxygen surged through his body.

As the air cleared his brain, he looked around. There it was. The chamber. His mother. Fighting the current, he pulled himself to shore and climbed out.

He knew he didn't have much time, so he hurried to the bed and reached out his hand. What had Jiménez told him he had to say?

"You came back," a voice said from behind him. "After I banned you."

Nick turned to find Seven Death glaring at him from across the river. "I found my own way," he said.

"It's too late," the death god said, splitting into two men. "You already failed."

Nick lunged toward his mom, but Seven Death split into all seven of his forms. Each of them moved to block Nick from his mother.

"How would you like to die?" asked one of them. "An arrow through the heart?"

Nick backed against the foot of the bed. He had to find a way to get to his mom. Then he remembered: *the item of power*. That was supposed to let him get past the demons.

But what was it?

"An ax to the throat?" another of the Seven Deaths said, stepping toward him.

Nick threw open a nearby chest, looking for anything that might be the item. Something personal that would have had great significance to the king's aunt. A crown maybe, or jewels? He pawed through necklaces, but none of them seemed right.

"Or would you like me to rip your heart straight out of your chest?"

A collection of intricately carved figurines sat on a shelf near the bed. He touched each of them, but nothing happened. He saw a wooden rack covered with beautiful gowns and headdresses. Clothes probably meant a lot to a queen. He flipped through them all, making sure to touch each one. But none of them had any effect.

Nick looked around the room, trying to buy time. Shoes. His mom certainly liked shoes, and there were dozens of pairs on the floor next to the bed. Slippers, boots, low moccasin-type things. There were too many valuable things to choose from.

"She's my mom. You can't have her."

"We already do," all the Seven Deaths said together.

The figure on the bed sat up and opened her glowing green eyes.

"Awilix," the death gods said, bowing before her. "What is your wish?"

"Gather my servants," the woman who still looked like Nick's mother said. "It is time to leave our tomb behind—and feed."

"As you command," the Seven Deaths said. "And what shall we do with the boy?"

Awilix looked Nick in the eyes, and the power of her gaze sent ice from the top of his head to the soles of his feet. But wasn't there a part of his mom inside? A part of her that might recognize him? Desperately he stared

246

at her, trying to make contact with whatever part of his mom still existed.

Her gaze locked on his. For a moment he thought he saw a glimmer of recognition. Then he remembered all his doubts. He'd never done any of the things she liked. He'd never asked her about her life before him. He spent his entire life expecting her to do things for him. How could she possibly want to protect him now?

She smiled. "Kill him."

"No!" Nick screamed. He looked for some place to run, but the death gods had him blocked off. Weapons raised, they closed in on him.

"Welcome to Xibalba," one of them said, raising his ax.

Nick spun back toward Awilix. "Please, Mom," he begged. "I know I've been a lousy son. Even if you can't do anything to stop this, I want to say I'm sorry for all the trouble I've put you through. All the dumb stuff I've done. I love you."

Awilix started to turn away from him and then stopped. Her head turned back. She raised a trembling hand, slapped it back down to her side, and tried to raise it again. It was like part of her was reaching out to him while the other fought against it.

Slowly, three words forced themselves out of her mouth. "Let. Him. Go."

"Awilix?" All of the Seven Deaths turned toward the goddess.

Her eyes met Nick's, and for just a brief moment, he saw his mom fighting against the power of the goddess with everything she had. Her gaze swept past Nick to the wall behind him, and then the goddess returned.

"Kill him!" she roared.

Nick's mind raced. What was that look? Had his mom been trying to tell him something?

As the Seven Deaths leaped toward him, Nick spun around. He searched the wall, and there it was, right where it had been the whole time. He'd been searching for all the things a member of Mayan royalty might find important, without ever thinking about the fact that the king's aunt was a woman, just like his mom.

In fact, in a way, he guessed she was kind of a mom too. Hadn't she raised the young king?

Diving forward, he reached out and grabbed the painting of a man and a woman holding a child. All at once he knew he was the most important thing in his mom's life. And to the aunt and uncle, the boy hadn't been a king. He'd been their child.

As Nick's fingers brushed across the child's face, an

explosion shook the chamber. Green light shot off the walls and ceiling. He held up the painting and all seven incarnations of the death lord fell back before him.

Rushing to his mom, he threw his arms around the glowing green goddess. "I love you, Mom. Come home."

For a moment the body he pressed against was ice-cold. Then he felt warm arms wrap around him. "I love you too."

CHAPTER 26

¿ESTO ES VERDADERAMENTE EL FINAL?

IS THIS REALLY THE END?

"I'm still not sure I understand why we're leaving three days early," Mom said as the men from the camp piled their luggage onto the top of the four-wheel-drive.

It was the morning after Nick had freed his mom from the power of the Mayan goddess, and she didn't seem to remember anything about it at all. He figured that was probably a good thing.

"You hit your head," he said. "Don't you remember?"

Mom reached up and felt the bandage on the front of her head with a look of mild surprise. "Oh, that's right. I guess I forgot. Everything's a little bit fuzzy." She looked at Dad as the two of them climbed into the car. "Did *you* know I hit my head?"

Dad pushed his Indiana Jones hat back on his head, looking a little confused. "I . . . *think* so."

"You got food poisoning," Carter said. "You know, the runs? You've been kind of out of it too."

Dad nodded slowly. "The curse of Montezuma's revenge, huh?"

Angelo shuddered. "Let's not talk about curses."

"The good news is, we get three days all expenses paid at the hotel," Nick said as he, Carter, and Angelo climbed into the car.

Mom leaned forward, looking at the man driving their car. "What happened to that nice Mr. Jiménez who brought us here?"

Nick glanced back at the Mexican police who were just finishing up their interviews. "He's telling some people all about how he ended up with certain artifacts. I wouldn't be surprised if he ends up being on TV."

Dr. Lopez and Dr. Canul had gone to great lengths explaining that Mr. Jiménez and a small group of his associates had planned an elaborate attempt to steal valuable artifacts that belonged in the country's museums. Dr. Canul still wasn't entirely certain on what had happened the night before. But Dr. Lopez had made it clear that it would be best for his career if he didn't mention the glowing green goddess. Considering that his father's career had been destroyed by odd beliefs, it wasn't a hard sell.

"That's nice," Mom said. "He seemed like a prince of a guy."

"The problem is he thought he was a king," Carter whispered.

As the driver pulled out of the camp, Nick took one last look at the pyramid where they had nearly ended up spending the rest of their lives—and after-lives.

"I wish I could have spent more time talking to the lords of death," Angelo said.

"Are you kidding?" Nick asked. "Those were, like, the freakiest guys I've ever met."

"Not to mention that they tried to kill us," Carter added.

Nick shook his head. Sometimes Angelo was just plain nuts. "Do you still think your parents are going to make you give up monster hunting?"

"I think we can come to some kind of agreement," Angelo said. He reached into his notebook and pulled out a slip of paper.

"What's that?" Nick asked. "It looks like one of

those DNA reports out of your tester."

"Not just any report," Angelo said. "This is the DNA result for One Death."

Nick and Carter stared at him. "How?" Nick asked. "You said you used all your swabs."

Angelo gave a sly smile. "I did. But remember when I grabbed his hand in the underworld? Just before we had to name the demons?"

Nick nodded.

"I scraped some skin from his palm with my fingernail. I ran the tests as soon as we got back."

"And?" Nick asked.

"Definitely not human."

"You are a crazy man," Carter said before going back to his knitting.

Nick noticed Carter had given up the hat he'd been working on. "Something new?" he asked.

Carter held up his project. "It's next year's Halloween costume. I'm going to be the Flying Scab."

Nick's dad turned around. "What are you boys going to do when we get back to the hotel?"

"I'm eating till I pop," Carter said.

Angelo pulled out his monster notebook. "I think I'll try to find the library. I've always wanted to learn more about *chupacabras*."

253

"What about you?" Nick's mom asked him. "Finally going to get that swim?"

Nick shook his head. "Actually, I was hoping you might teach me some Spanish."

Back So Soon?

How was your trip? Nick, Carter, and Angelo seem to have survived. Of course, they always do. I'm thinking about taking a little trip myself. Perhaps to visit my mother. It's been a while since I've seen her, and for some reason I feel the need just now.

Will I be back? Perhaps. Although the boys seem to be growing up. Maybe it's time they got on without me. And what about you? Are there adventures you've been meaning to take? Dark and shadowy haunts calling out to you?

Go now, at once. Before it's too late. Perhaps your story will be in my next case file.

Or perhaps you'll start a case file of your own.

Sincerely,
B. B.

Facts and Myths

One of the best things about writing a series like Case File 13 is that I get to find lots of fun facts about interesting topics like pyramids, Mayan temples, and ancient writings. I combine those with legends, myths, and rumors, and stir it all together with things I make up from my own imagination.

The first thing I discovered when I began researching *Curse of the Mummy's Uncle* is that the Mayans were and are an amazing people. The ancient Mayans are known for their art, architecture, math, and astronomy, among other things. Because Mayan script has been mostly deciphered, we can read about 90 percent of their ancient writings. That helps us understand a lot about their lives and beliefs.

The second thing I learned is that pyramids are awesome. Although we tend to think of Egypt when we think of pyramids, there are actually hundreds of them spread all over the world. Many Mayan cities, including Tikal, Yaxha, and Ixlu, have what are called twin-pyramid groups where two pyramids were built on the east and west side of a plaza.

Mayan pyramids often had temples on top. The pyramids represented mountains and the temples represented caves to the underworld. Passages were sometimes dug down from the temple into the pyramid, where royalty was buried. Many times the doors to these passages are carved to look like the mouths of monsters.

The names of the demons I used in this book all come from Mayan mythology. (Even the Flying Scab!) The *Popol Vuh* is a real document that includes the story of the Hero Twins, Xbalanque and Hunahpu. Almost all the tests the boys have to get through are the same ones the Hero Twins have to pass. (Except for the Whac-A-Mole skeletons. I made that up because it seemed so funny.) Xibalba is actually what the Mayans called the underworld, and it does translate to "place of fear."

While I used lots of facts, I also made a lot up. None of the characters are real. The archaeological site is not a real location. There is no pyramid called Xma' Su'tal Hats'utsil. The ceremonies where Mayans of royal blood could pass through the underworld to become gods is made up from a little bit of fact and a little bit of legend, but mostly from my imagination. I totally invented the items of power.

Hopefully this adventure made you want to find out more about pyramids, Mayans, and Mesoamerican history. If so, there are lots of great books on the subjects from the real experts.

Here are just a few.

Baquedano, Elizabeth. *Aztec, Inca & Maya: Discover the World of the Aztecs, Incas, and Mayas—Their Beliefs, Rituals, and Civilizations*, rev. ed. DK Eyewitness Books. New York: DK Publishing, 2011.

Maloy, Jackie. *The Ancient Maya*. New York: Children's Press, 2010.

Matthews, Rupert. *You Wouldn't Want to Be a Mayan Soothsayer!: Fortunes You'd Rather Not Tell*. You Wouldn't Want To . . . New York: Franklin Watts, 2008.

You can also find plenty of information (along with some awesome pictures and videos) on the internet, too. Who knows, maybe you'll want to make up your own story of Mayan pyramids and what happens inside.

ACKNOWLEDGMENTS

It's not every day an author gets to share many of his childhood experiences with his readers. Especially not in a series that's as much fun to write as Case File 13. Special thanks to Michael Bourret, who helped make this dream come true; Andrew Harwell, who saw the stories I was trying to tell and made them so much better; Douglas Holgate, who brought my words to life with his amazing pictures; all the staff at Harper Children's who turned a story into what you now hold in your hands; to my family, who support me in too many ways to count; and most of all, to you, my readers, without whom none of the words would matter. It's been a great journey, and I hope you've enjoyed the series. Feel free to contact me at scott@jscottsavage.com and let me know how you liked it.

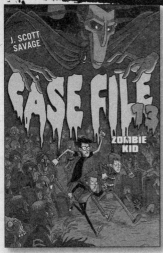